MERCURY RISING

Tin Can Mystery #1

Jerusha Jones

For more information about Jerusha Jones's other novels, please visit www.jerushajones.com

Cover design by Elizabeth Berry MacKenney.

CHAPTER 1

"Eva, I left three rolls of toilet paper in the cupboard under your bathroom sink," Sloane said. "And a roll of paper towels on the kitchen counter and a bottle of Windex—just until you find yours, you know. You have all that glass." She sounded breathless, reeling off items from the revolving checklist that perpetually resided in her mind. "We could order you a pizza, have it delivered. I'm so sorry we can't stay late to help you with those crazy instructions." In the background, Sloane's nine-month-old son objected mightily to being strapped into his car seat and her two little girls chattered in short piping tones.

I shook my head and grinned into the phone. It hadn't been more than five minutes since my sister and her family had left, and already her call sounded like a zoo in a minivan. "Thanks for everything. But no. Get your munchkins into bed and put up your feet. I'm an adult, which means I can handle assembling a few IKEA bookcases by myself."

Sloane snorted. "More power to you." There was a muffled interruption, and then she returned to the line. "Riley says to tell you that he stashed the toolbox with all the screwdrivers and hammer and stuff in the coat closet."

"Give him a big hug for me."

"Oh, I will." Sloane trilled off into her infectious laugh. "And more," she added huskily.

"La la la la la," I hollered. "TMI. But thanks." I hung up with a smile that was immediately replaced by a hefty sigh.

Boxes. I was sick of boxes. And all I could see were boxes, like cancerous growths heaped over the floors and against the walls of my new abode. Riley had insisted that they be dispersed evenly so the floating house (not a houseboat since it didn't have its own propulsion system) wouldn't list to port—or was it starboard?—with the extra unbalanced weight.

I had to climb over boxes to make my way to the kitchen. Like Sloane, I also had a mental checklist, and forging a clear path from room to room jumped to the top spot on it. Making up a bed for the night dropped to second place, mainly because I was certain I'd be able to fall asleep just tipped against a wall at this point.

Food had marquee billing, regardless. The offer of hot pizza made by someone else had been tempting, but if I relaxed for two seconds, there'd be no reviving my will to work—my muscles would seize up and not regain any sort of functional mobility until I'd had at least twelve hours of sleep.

During my supervision of the ragtag team of movers that afternoon, I'd nabbed a couple boxes of pantry items and loaded the contents into a cupboard. Tuna on saltines it would have to be. With green olives. Dinner of champions and the recently displaced.

But the upheaval in my life meant I now got to live within actual gossip-over-lunch distance from my sister. That I got to be a babysit-at-a-moment's-notice aunt to my nieces and nephew and to appreciate—or endure, depending on how you looked at it—my brother-in-law's quirky sense of humor firsthand.

Meals would also get much, much better than I'd had time for during the past several months. If only I could find the Le Creuset Dutch oven, not to mention a can opener. So close and yet so far—the tuna would have to wait. Instead, I doused the crackers with Tabasco sauce while I leaned over the kitchen sink and watched the sunset turn to magenta over the Willamette River's opposite shore through the window. Nothing like a little heartburn to keep a person productive late into the night.

~oOo~

The next morning, I rolled out of bed. Mainly because it took some strategic levering and deep breaths to get myself upright. But I'd made good progress the night before, demonstrated primarily by the fact that I'd actually slept between clean sheets on a fully assembled bed which happened to be located in the correct room.

The same could not be said for my clothing. But I eventually found the duffel bag full of jeans, T-shirts, underwear, and workout clothes that had made the cross-country trip stuffed behind the driver's seat of my old Volvo. For some reason, the bag had been wedged in the utility closet between the furnace and the hot water heater. Probably my oldest niece's idea of a logical spot for safekeeping. I remembered seeing her lug the thing along the dock, her silhouette puffed up to twice its normal size by the life jacket her father, mother, and I had all insisted she wear while she trooped back and forth like a cheerful little pack mule, her arms full of my possessions. The kid was a workaholic. It was in her DNA.

I pulled on a pair of stretchy pants and a tank top, then opened the glass French doors that led from my bedroom onto a wide stretch of wood-planked deck. It was that magic breath in time barely before sunrise when the world is just coming into focus. The river made little gurgling sounds as it rippled past the pilings my house was lashed to.

I stepped outside in my bare feet and flopped down a yoga mat. It was chilly and misty and must have rained in the night, although I'd been too comatose to hear raindrops plopping on the metal roof.

I cranked out the Five Tibetans, twenty-one repetitions of each, and savored the sensations of strength and limberness as my muscles warmed up. I don't truly practice yoga, but a lot of the yoga stretches and poses feel really good. The Five Tibetans had become my buddies during the uncertainty and insanely short deadlines that are typical in the world of high-tech but which become even worse when the company you work for has been sold for an astronomical sum to a group of power-hungry venture capitalists and is being restructured to capitalize their investment even further.

Who can even count that much money? Who even cares?

Not me, apparently, because I'd been laid off. And suddenly I'd had absolutely nothing to do except sign the stifling non-compete agreement that Kris, my friend and lunchtime power-walking pal from the human resources department, had slipped into my in-box so that I would qualify for a modest severance package. I found out later that she, too, had been laid off the next week, after she'd completed her duty of filing the termination paperwork for eighty percent of her coworkers. The whole thing had felt like a nosedive into the Grand Canyon.

I took it as a sign that it was also time to get the hell out of Dodge.

"Isn't that classy," said a whiny, adenoidal voice from the river. "Sticking your ass up in the air like that. Just what I wanted to see while I was communing with nature."

My downward-facing dog hit the deck so fast that the yoga mat did nothing to cushion the collision my knees had with the wood underneath. My eyes watered with the pain, and I ducked to peek underneath my elbow at the intruder.

She had violently blue hair that scraggled down to her shoulders and a little scrunched-up face with a chin that was tucked way back under her nose. Her hands were resting on the shaft of a double-bladed paddle which was balanced across the bow of a neon-orange kayak.

She must be really good at maneuvering that kayak, because I hadn't heard her approach. I pivoted to sitting cross-legged on the yoga mat and studied her. "I know you. At least, I recognize you."

"That would be my Great Bluedini Kool-Aid hair."

I nodded. "Hard to miss. I suppose it's on par—speaking of nature—with my having my ass in the air."

The girl snorted. With one quick flick of her paddle, her kayak bumped up against my deck, and she stuck out her hand—the fingers of which were tipped with turquoise nail polish—like the grownup she wasn't yet. "Willow Ratliff. You signed a moorage lease with my grandmother yesterday."

I shook the proffered hand. "Eva Fairchild."

"I know. I do Gran's filing. Otherwise nothing would get filed and some stupid auditor would have a heyday with her. Which means I also know your driver's license number, your social security number, that you're currently unemployed, the name of your last employer, and your previous address. D.C. huh? What's it like? What'd you do there?"

I blinked. There was no way I could tell this punk child that I'd worked in the security industry. I'd be a justifiable laughing stock forever. So instead, I told her the other part of the truth. "Vicious. Like a bunch of zombies dressed up in expensive suits who live in concrete bunkers and only come out when it's time to eat money."

Willow snorted again, but differently. The sound seemed to be a significant, and rather expressive, part of her vocabulary. "I don't go for that apocalyptic dystopian junk. I'm into near-future space opera."

Was this some kind of contest? I had no idea how to answer her. So I shrugged and said, "I'm into béchamel, velouté, espagnole, hollandaise, and tomate."

That earned me a squint and even more scrunching of the little face. "Huh. At least you're more interesting than the old miser who lived here before. Don't let Doc catch you with your ass in the air. He'd think it was a suggestion." She shoved off and paddled smoothly away.

A pair of raucous, darting birds with wide white bands across their throats streaked overhead, slinging insults at each other like a pair of arguing lovers. Cottonwoods on the bank shivered in the almost nonexistent breeze, and a spreading warm glow rose above the eastern dike, turning the river from inky blue to sparkling in a matter of moments.

Despite Willow's esoteric perspective on genre fiction, she had the right idea about observing nature. One of the things I was most looking forward to about living here was experiencing nature up close and personal, bobbing on the river, buffeted by the wind, and hopefully not drowning. I wanted—no, I needed—to learn how to manage a kayak by myself. And to obtain a field guide to Pacific Northwest birds pronto.

An army of one showed up as I was gnawing on a Clif bar for breakfast—Sloane.

"Riley's taking the kids to the science museum for a little daddy time, and to keep them out of our hair. So we can really bust our chops today," she announced as she sidled through the front door past me, several reusable grocery bags hanging from each arm. "What are you eating? Yuck. And you—" She stuck out her tongue at me. "Of all people, you should know that a proper breakfast is mandatory." She giggled. "I also knew you wouldn't have found your supplies yet. Hey, paths." She waltzed along the trail I'd cleared through the living room. "Am I a terrific sister, or what?" she asked as she plunked the bags on the kitchen counter and turned her happy smile and glittery green eyes toward me.

I couldn't help grinning back. "Yes."

Sloane freed her arms from the bag handles and wrapped herself in a tight hug. She bounced on her toes. "I just can't believe it still," she squealed. "I'm going to make myself a nuisance before I do fully believe it. You're really here. Like old times, before you went away to college."

There are eight years between Sloane and me. I'm older. Technically, we're half-sisters. We look nothing alike because we take after our different mothers with regard to coloring and complexion, but we both inherited our father's tall and lanky physique. Sloanie has filled hers out a little more than I have, probably because she's a mother herself. But she's still gorgeous, maybe even more than back in the days when she modeled. She was never a big league supermodel; mostly she posed for in-house department store labels and home furnishings ads. Her heart never was in the glitz and itinerancy of that lifestyle, so I hadn't been surprised when she'd opted to quit and put her paralegal training to work instead.

Neither had I been surprised that Riley Tillman had been gobsmacked by the bombshell who'd been sent by the temp agency to fill a vacancy at his small firm. He'd won Sloanie's heart and put a ring on her finger before her six-month contract was up. And now they were busy making and raising beautiful babies.

I crossed the kitchen quickly and wrapped Sloane in a hug of my own. "I'm not a phantom. Which means you can hug me, like, for real, instead of pretending. I'm having a little trouble soaking in the reality myself. What did you bring to eat?"

Sloane started pawing through the bags and pulled out a container of Greek yogurt and little tubs of dates, pecans, and coconut.

"Oh boy," I groaned.

"What did I tell you?" Sloane winked at me. "This is going to be soooo great, us living near each other. What do you think of the house?"

"Smaller. I need your help downsizing." I grunted as I ripped the foil off the yogurt container. "Which I'd wanted to do anyway. I just didn't have time to get rid of the stuff I don't need before the move. But perfect, otherwise. I love the view and how quiet it is. I met a neighbor already this morning. She referred to the previous owner as a miser."

Sloane laughed and opened packages of plastic bowls and plastic spoons. "That's an understatement. He pinched his emotions as well as his pennies. His relatives hated him. They just wanted whatever cash could be wrangled out of the estate without having to deal with it themselves, which is why they hired Riley's partner to handle probate on their behalf. He was happy I lined up a buyer so fast."

"Isn't that a conflict of interest?" I sprinkled dates and nuts into my bowl.

"Nope. Generally, floating houses are in demand in the Portland real estate market, but this one's odd." Sloane snickered. "Seeing as how it's made out of a few shipping containers stuck together. People immediately imagine rusty sheet metal with big letters spelling *Hanjin* or *COSCO* on the side. About the same as living in a sewer to their way of thinking. The real estate agents he tried to list it with pretty much laughed in his face."

"But it's nothing like that," I spluttered, then paused. "Well, maybe it needs some paint."

"Cosmetics," Sloane agreed before shoveling a spoonful of yogurt in her mouth. "I knew you'd see the diamond in the rough."

CHAPTER 2

I clutched my bowl of chickpea and mint salad, stood on my doorstep for a moment, and took a deep breath. The little bony twig of a woman with a smooth, chin-length bob of flaming orange hair had given me directions to her house at the other end of the marina. The passage involved several left turns along floating walkways and crossing through the locked gate that split the marina into its north and south halves. How hard could it be? I already had the numerical code for unlocking the gate memorized.

The way she'd described the marina community's de rigueur habit of holding a welcome party for each new resident—tag, you're it!—had almost hinted that I'd also be navigating from the slum side to the posh side in order to attend. Or maybe I'd read her wrong. After all, she'd had to crane her neck way back to peer into my face. Maybe that much stretching had altered her normal tone of voice into a sort of breathless snootiness.

Besides giving Willow a run for her money in the unnatural hair color department, Bettina Godinou, my distant-north neighbor, had also been dressed in sleek black designer togs and bejeweled on just about every visible digit plus earlobes plus neck. She was a walking, clanking, jangling costume jewelry exhibit. You could hear her both coming and going from several yards away. But maybe noise carries farther over water.

After Bettina had stopped by with her invitation and spent an additional several minutes ogling my sprawl of unpacked possessions with the air of one sent on a reconnoitering mission, Sloane had started chuckling to herself but refusing to offer any sort of analysis on this unexpected bolt of hospitality.

"Spit it out," I finally grumbled.

"You're so in for it now," she'd tittered. "I want a full report tomorrow. You're going to learn that people in the Portland area are a little bit different. Flavorful. Whimsical."

"Alien?"

Sloanie released her pent-up laughter in a prolonged peal. "That too. It's nothing like where we grew up."

Meaning submerged in stodgy East Coast middle-aged money. The Fairchilds weren't Old Money by any means—because it hadn't all been spent yet. Dad was far from an aristocratically veneered pauper. He was still making deals and rolling around in the dough pretty thick. He was also on his sixth wife. Sloanie and I had given up counting all the girlfriends who'd been slotted between the wives. Sometimes we barely learned the first names of the wives before they absconded with a chunk of Dad's spare change and a house of their own in the next divorce.

Dad certainly loved women. Or maybe it was that he didn't know what to do with himself without them. I guess it had been a good thing, then, that he'd gotten daughters out of his first and third matrimonial entanglements. He'd actually been a semi-decent father when he was around; he'd just been distracted most of the time. Still was. Sloane and I had learned to leave him alone, and he returned the favor. Maybe at Christmas I'd let him know about my change of address.

But Sloane and I had made tremendous progress on the domestic front. My living room and kitchen were now relatively tidy and uncluttered, and the bedroom was getting close. We'd also given every room a thorough disinfecting. I didn't want old-miser cooties thinking they could recolonize my property. We'd also found the closest grocery store and replaced the refrigerated staples that I'd had to toss out in D.C. because they couldn't make the trip.

My calves were tight from all the hiking. When you live in a floating house, it's not like you can park in an attached garage. Nothing's attached. Every trip to an outside source involves a trek along a floating walkway and up a gangplank to the parking lot and back again. We'd hauled umpteen armfuls of flattened cardboard to the recycling dumpster and borrowed the marina's wheeled carts to take my excess stuff up to Sloane's minivan.

When she'd driven away to make a donation at the local Goodwill on my behalf before heading home, her van had been riding very low on its rear axle. We'd been brutal in paring down my possessions, and I was feeling as though a giant load had been lifted.

So hefting the salad bowl for a long walk across the marina was a mere pittance. I could do this charming sociability thing. Totally. Yep. I took another deep breath and set off, my footsteps reverberating on the floating walkway.

Bettina's house was an exact personification of its owner. I'd never seen so many lawn ornaments in my life.

Especially considering she didn't even have a lawn. Whirligigs, weather vanes, optical illusion spinning deely-bobs, tattered windsocks of zero practical value. Why have flowers in the half-whiskey-barrel planters that clog your decks when you can stake all sorts of gaudy bits of colored plastic and metal in them instead?

I stepped over the watery gap between the walkway and the platform on which Bettina's house was built and conked my head on a hunk of driftwood that dangled from one of the wind chimes lining the shallow entry to her house.

"You're tall." Bettina emerged from the doorway and stood on her tiptoes to inspect the driftwood for damage. "I told you that you didn't need to bring anything."

It was the one instruction she'd given me which I'd intentionally ignored. Maybe I was being passive-aggressive, but I also knew better than to show up at a party empty-handed. I just smiled down at her.

She'd changed clothes. She was now clad in a filmy, tent-like, leopard-print tunic over leopard-print leggings and gold sandals. She was wearing enough stiff gold collar necklaces and bracelets to give King Tutankhamun a case of green envy.

She pivoted back into the open doorway and clapped her hands. The hubbub of conversations inside fell silent. "Everyone," she said in a shockingly loud voice for such a little person, "this is Eva." Then she performed a swirly motion with her hands and ended up pointing both forefingers at me with a wide-eyed look that indicated I was now expected to do something phenomenal.

Instead, I peeked around the door frame into Bettina's living room and gave a slight wave to the crowd gathered there. I was pulled inside by eager hands, and people clamored over the top of each other to introduce themselves. To say I was smothered would be an understatement. There was absolutely nothing snooty about the welcome I received.

Someone relieved me of the salad bowl and replaced it with a plastic tumbler of fruit punch. I anxiously glanced around at the walls for a maximum occupancy sign. I was pretty sure we were exceeding it. I checked the floor between my feet for rapidly developing puddles, to see if the overloaded house was taking on water, but the sisal rug seemed dry.

Little bird-like hands wrapped around my elbow, and Bettina steered me through the throng accompanied by a constant stream of names and short descriptions of the boats or floating houses that correlated with the people she was pointing out. Her monologue went something like this:

"The young man in the corner looking downtrodden is Ancer Potts. Whatever he says to you, just nod. Chances are good you won't understand it. I know I don't. He's some kind of genius and lives in the deathtrap sailboat covered in blue tarps one row over from you in B-4. There's my good friend, Petula Dibble, filling the pitcher at the sink. Her husband, Boris, is around here somewhere, probably inspecting my roof. He thinks I need a new one. They're my next door neighbors but one. You passed their place at E-15. Oh, look, Marcy's here. That girl travels so much, I didn't know if she'd get my note in time or not. She's a geologist and has that tidy little cruiser berthed at the base of the gangplank from the office." Et cetera, et cetera, et cetera.

The stream of information quickly overflowed what little mental capacity I had available. But as I gazed down at the top of the bright-orange head skimming along beside me, I realized tiny Bettina was the undisputed social maven of the community. Apparently, I had passed inspection earlier and was now in the induction phase.

Bettina finally released me out on the rear deck where there was actual open standing room and a gentle breeze. She aimed a knuckly be-ringed finger at the stout, grizzled man who was overseeing the barbecue grill. "No pinching." She tugged on my elbow, forcing me to bend my ear down near her mouth to hear her breathy whisper. "His name is Doc Perlmutter, but he is in no way qualified to examine you—in any capacity. If he claims otherwise, you have free license to knee him in the gonads." She fired another warning scowl at Doc and slipped back inside the house.

He offered a toothy smile amid the couldn't-be-bothered-to-shave sandy-brown-and-gray stubble that covered the bottom half of his face and his neck and the area of his wide chest that was visible beneath his partially unbuttoned shirt. It was definitely not an attractive look, but I suspected he thought the extra hair masked his wrinkles or demonstrated virility or something. He had a weather-beaten visage with pronounced eye bags which was at the opposite end of the spectrum from what I consider handsome ruggedness. It didn't help that he lifted a plastic tumbler and winked at me over the top of it before tossing back the rest of his drink.

My unpleasant train of thought—namely, why on earth had Bettina abandoned me out here with this lug?—was interrupted by an expressive snort. I turned to find Willow peeking at me from under the brim of a voluminous newsboy cap. Every strand of her blue hair was carefully tucked up into the cap and completely hidden from view. She was wedged in between two

Adirondack chairs at the corner of the deck, leaning against the railing with her own tumbler of punch balanced on the flat railing cap.

I sidled up to her. "Rescue me?" I whispered.

"I'm technically not supposed to be here," she whispered back. "Adults only. But Bettina's right. Ol' Doc will leave you alone if you put up a fuss. He prefers the stupid, gooey kind of women who drape all over him rather than vice versa."

"Wait," I said, understanding dawning. "Is he the one you warned me about this morning, when my ass was in the air?"

Willow grinned. "Couldn't let a sister down. There's a sort of collusion here at the marina. The girls look after each other when Doc's around."

It wasn't exactly a warm fuzzy feeling, this knowledge. But it functioned like another notch of acceptance in my new world. Welcome aboard, warts and all.

I nodded, completely content to have a private conversation with a world-wise teenager—and to leave Doc to his own devices with the seasoning salt and spatula at the other end of the deck. "What's so adult about this party?"

Willow lifted her tumbler and pitched an eyebrow at me. "I take it you haven't had a sip yet."

I sniffed at my cup first, and it was enough—the vapors just about peeled my eyeballs. "Whew. Do you think it will kill any fish if I dump this in the river?"

Willow chuckled. "At least they'll die happy." She squinted into her own cup at the inch of punch glowing fruitily in the bottom. Her tone of voice changed, and she wouldn't look at me when she asked, "You got a problem with alcohol?"

A bit of a tricky subject when you're talking with a kid who's maybe only two-thirds of the way to the legal drinking age. "No. I just don't like what it does to people. My mom drove herself straight into a tree while she was under the influence. I'm kind of bitter about that."

"No kidding."

I couldn't tell if Willow's comment was a question or an offer of commiseration. But she was looking at me now, her pale gray eyes watery at the edges. There was a little pucker between her brows.

"No kidding," I confirmed. "I was three."

"Were you in the car with her?"

"Nope. I'd been left at home with the nanny."

"Shit." Willow slowly tipped her cup and we both watched the vile golden liquid dribble into the water below.

"Pretty much," I agreed.

"All right, my beauties," Doc hollered. "Chow time."

We followed him inside. It would have been nearly impossible not to since the platter he carried drifted aromatic bratwurst and burger scents in its wake. My stomach growled in anticipation.

There was a crush around the buffet arranged on the island in Bettina's kitchen as we heaped paper plates full of typical end-of-summer fare—grilled meats, cold salads, sliced veggies fresh from a local farmer's garden, potato chips, and watermelon wedges. I found a squishy perch at the end of a sofa and balanced my plate on my knees while conversations swirled around me. Fortunately, no one required my participation in dialogue, and I got to observe and learn and salt away tidbits of information to ponder later.

Willow had claimed a squat, padded footstool next to a recliner on the other side of the room, and every once in a while she'd make eye contact with me and we'd share a knowing grin. In spite of her attempt at a disguise—such as it was—so she could sneak into the party, I got the impression that her presence didn't really bother anyone, that they were tolerating her, maybe even protecting her, keeping an eye out for her like a rather dysfunctional band of guardian angels. She made no further raids on the punch bowl that I could see.

My backside grew tingly from sitting immobile while my body was folded at awkward angles in the tight quarters. When we were kids, Sloane and I had come up with a name for the condition: TB, which stood for *Tired Bottom*. We'd whisper to each other about our degrees of TB and giggle, which helped pass the time while the grownups droned on and on. TB is still my most reliable social barometer. When I have reached the completely numb stage, I figure I've spent an acceptable length of time in the company of others and allow myself to make my good-byes and exit stage right.

Bettina and her friend, Petula, were in the kitchen consolidating the leftovers and shrouding everything perishable with plastic wrap.

"Your salad was delicious." Petula slurped the few remaining chickpeas off the serving spoon and dropped it into the sink. "What's in the dressing?"

"Lemon zest and juice, olive oil, fresh mint, minced garlic, kosher salt, red pepper flakes. Pretty simple," I replied with a grin and reached for my empty bowl.

But Bettina was faster than I was. She grabbed the bowl and whipped it behind her back.

"It doesn't need to be clean," I protested. "I'll just stick it in the dishwasher at my house." I waved toward the piles of serving dishes already surrounding the sink awaiting their turn in the sudsy water. "You have enough work ahead of you. It was a lovely party. Thank you."

Bettina shook her head vehemently, sending the necklaces clanking against each other. "Guests of honor do not wash their own dishes. It's one of my rules. In fact, I'm going to hold your bowl hostage until you come over for dinner and meet my son."

Behind her, Petula nodded with wide-eyed encouragement. "You should," she mouthed.

I frowned at both of them.

"He's decent looking, has a regular job, and he's tall enough for you," Bettina continued. "A little grouchy sometimes, but you seem like a woman who could tolerate that. Not too chatty yourself, are you?"

The two women smiled up at me hopefully. Apparently there was more than one kind of collusion going on around here.

So the evening had been dual-purposed—a neighborhood meet-and-greet *and* an audition for matrimonial prospects with a man whose mother I had only just met. Fabulous.

I wondered if he knew what she was plotting. Probably. I doubted this was her first attempt, and she certainly wasn't subtle, which could account for his alleged grouchiness.

I gave the appearance of surrender—waved cheerily and backed away, wending my way through the remaining partiers, and found the front door by myself. I'm an old hand at this sort of social finagling. It would be fine—maybe even optimal—to let Bettina think she'd won this particular battle. I'd managed to avoid marriage so far, so I had every confidence in my ability to out-persevere her.

Potential mothers-in-law were usually desperate, which made their attention spans rather spastic. The next cutie in a skirt who happened to walk by would be just as interesting to Bettina as I was. It would be easy to disappear once a suitable distraction (unknowingly) presented herself. I was just one in a long line of many, and readily forgotten.

I strolled through the widely spaced pools of light from the lampposts bolted to the edges of the walkways, enjoying the balmy evening. Until footsteps thumped rapidly behind me, and Willow wheezed, "Hey, wait up."

"As long as you're not Doc come to pinch me goodnight," I muttered.

Willow replied with one of her expressive snorts. "He did seem to be on his best behavior tonight. But that doesn't mean you can let down your guard." She pulled up even with me and flashed a scrunchy grin from under the cap. "Actually, Bettina's son is kind of hunky. I'd go for him if I were thirty years older."

And there you have it, ladies and gentlemen, a raving endorsement from a kid with satellite dishes for ears. I groaned. "More collusion?"

"Nope." Willow made a show of swiping her palms across each other several times. "My part's done. I wash my hands of it. Totally in your court now."

But I was ready for a change in subject. I stood to the side and waited while Willow punched in the code and pushed open the creaky metal mesh gate. After I'd stepped through behind her and the gate had swung closed with a satisfying clang, I said, "Since I got all mushy earlier and told you about my mom, I'm gonna exercise my right to be nosy and ask where yours is."

It wasn't exactly a fair, tit-for-tat type of assumption, but I was hoping she'd fall for it. And she did.

"Prison," she answered with a little shrug. She stuffed her hands in her jeans pockets and hunched her shoulders as though she was engrossed with watching the tips of her sneakers strike forward with every step.

Somehow, the death of a parent seemed less heartbreaking. I was glad the falling dusk hid the expression of surprise and pity that must have swept across my face before I could carefully rearrange my features.

"She likes to cook too," Willow continued with a forced perkiness. "I looked up those words you used earlier. The five mother sauces of French cuisine. Except my mom cooked meth. Lots of it. Plus possession with intent to distribute. Three strikes and all that. I won't see her again until I'm twenty-two, unless I go visit her in prison."

I'm not a fan of vulgar profanity—or elegant profanity, for that matter—but it's appropriate in some situations. I tried to keep my voice neutral as I echoed Willow's earlier sentiment. "Shit."

"Pretty much," she agreed.

She scuffed along for a full minute in silence, then stopped and peered up at me. "Can I ask you for a gigantic favor? All Gran and I eat comes from boxes and bottles. Do you know what those additives and chemicals are doing to my organs and brain? Besides the fact that my family already has a chemical problem. I'm sure you noticed that Gran smokes like there's no tomorrow and like her head's not a giant hair spray bomb. I'm going to get Alzheimer's for sure. Early onset. It's probably already started." She yanked off her cap, and her blue hair tumbled down in a tangled mass. "Can you teach me how to cook real food? Like that salad you made—and other stuff?"

There is only one right answer to such an appeal. But I tried to pretend it wasn't momentous—at least to me—and shrugged back at her. "Sure. But I have two rules. You have to eat what you make, and you have to clean up your own mess."

Willow's grin was a reward in itself. She stuck out her hand like the grown-up she still wasn't. "Deal."

We shook on it.

And then something broke the reflected light beam of a lamppost on the water in my peripheral vision. It made sloshy sounds as it bumped gently against the walkway with the river current.

Willow caught a glimpse of it too. "People are always dumping their junk in the water," she muttered. "Looks like a tarp." She stooped to grab at the sodden fabric but suddenly froze in an open pike position, teetering on the edge of the walkway. She emitted a strangled shriek before vomiting all over the place.

I caught her before she fell and hauled her back to safety.

But in the process, I also captured a fleeting, jolting impression, and it was enough. That thing in the water. It wasn't a tarp.

CHAPTER 3

We weren't more than forty feet from my front door. Willow was a limp weight in my arms, moaning incoherently. I dragged her along the walkway and propped her against me while I unlocked the door. By then she'd recovered enough mobility to be able to stagger into the living room.

I aimed her toward the sofa then found a plastic storage tub, dumped out the art supplies it held, and shoved it under her chin. "If you need to throw up again, use this."

"Oh man, oh man—man, oh man," she moaned and rolled onto her back with her knees up, cradling the tub on her belly. "Oh man."

I leaned over her and brushed her hair away from her face. "Yeah, it was a man. I have to go back out there, Willow. You stay right here. I mean it. Unless you need the bathroom, which is just off the kitchen." I clicked on a few lights for Willow, snatched the flashlight I'd tucked on the top shelf in the coat closet, and grabbed my phone off the kitchen counter.

Oh man, oh man, oh man—my thoughts echoed Willow's as my feet pounded on the sturdy boards of the walkway.

He was still there, three-quarters submerged and face down. I didn't know how Willow and I both recognized it was a man. There must have been intuitive clues we'd picked up on, but I was in no condition to be able to articulate them at the moment. The best I could do was listen to the subtle buzzing as my call to 911 rang and the monotone voice of a dispatcher answered.

What was my emergency? The lady on the line wanted to know.

"Uh, there's a man," I croaked. "In the water. At Marten's Marina."

I squeezed my eyes shut and tried to picture the map I'd followed across the country to the little corner in the upper left portion of Oregon, to my new home. The names of the surrounding small towns, the street address for the marina—all were elusive at the moment. Couldn't 911 triangulate the location of a cell phone call?

"Northwest of Portland proper, on the Willamette River, close to the Columbia. Do you know where I mean?" My mouth was gluey, as though my tongue was working around gobs of rubber cement.

The operator recited an address to me. It sounded familiar.

"They don't need to hurry," I added. "He's dead."

That part I probably could articulate—a complete checklist of reasons why there was no urgency about pulling the man out of the water, no reason for me to apply my rusty knowledge of CPR—but the 911 operator didn't stick around for the particulars. Once she'd confirmed that I would stay at the scene and was in decent health myself, she told me a police officer would be in touch and clicked off.

Which was probably a good thing, because now my brain was babbling, clamoring all over itself, even though my vocal cords and lips hadn't engaged yet. And per usual, they wouldn't. The panicky terror was restricted to inside my head, where it belonged.

I played the shaky flashlight beam over the sodden mass of clothing in the water. The man's jacket had billowed up across his back and shoulders, and the confined gasses were what seemed to be making him float. His head hung so low that I could only see the tips of his hair—of indistinct color in the greenish-brackish water—waving in the current below the surface. The white, bloated fingers of his left hand dimpled in the light, giving me my first indicator of why I'd known it was a man.

His knuckles. Even though his skin was waterlogged, the puffiness couldn't mask the fact that his knuckles were man-sized, enlarged from hard work and maybe the beginnings of arthritis. No wedding ring.

Blobs of Willow's vomit floated around him, and I had a sudden urge to hose off the walkway so the evidence of her distress wouldn't be obvious to the responding officers. But I'd watched enough cop shows on television to know not to disturb the scene any more than it already had been. Although it was clear the man hadn't died here. The algae-covered pilings and blocks of Styrofoam that supported the walkway were just his washed-up final resting location.

And then I got cold. Bone-marrow-cringing cold. My teeth rattled in my head. I drew up my limbs just as Willow had, and sat rocking on the walkway, wrapped into the tiniest ball I could manage.

Red and blue flashing lights arrived in the parking lot. A car door slammed, and the gangplank clanged with hurried footsteps behind a sweeping flashlight beam.

He found me quickly. It probably helped that my party-appropriate sundress was a cheerful yellow floral print. I must have stood out like a bright beacon hunkered halfway down the A row boardwalk.

A pair of scuffed black boots thumped to a stop beside me. Then a heavy, warm hand on my shoulder and a mellow male voice. "You call this in?"

I tried to nod.

"How you doing?"

"Okay," I squeaked.

His hand shifted to my elbow, and he helped me stand. As I unfolded, I knew he was eyeing my legs even though he was trying not to. They were covered in goose bumps, just like the rest of my body. My dress ran short, as all dresses do on me. Unfortunately, there was quite a bit of leg available for viewing at the moment. Right next to a corpse.

"You live here?" he asked.

I managed an honest-to-goodness, qualified nod this time and tried to smile into his serious blue eyes, which fell about an inch below mine. He was resplendent in equipment—radio clipped to his shoulder, badge, stuff bulging all his pockets, and a belt that was so laden with a gun and other gadgets that it hung low on his hips. His name tag said *Webber*.

"I need to secure the area, and then we'll have to wait until a whole bunch of people get here. Do you have a comfortable place to bide the time?" He'd barely even glanced at the dead guy. Maybe he was worried about having another type of emergency on his hands.

"My house." I waved vaguely behind me.

He escorted me along the walkway and poked his head in through the front door opening, quickly scanning my living room. "You'll stay here until someone can talk to you?"

"Sure."

"It'd be a good idea to drink something. Not alcohol though," he offered. "Put your feet up." He gave me a conspiratorial wink—nothing like the leering affront Doc had perpetrated earlier—then was gone just as quickly, leaving me feeling much warmer and immeasurably relieved. The poor floater was now someone else's responsibility.

Willow was nowhere to be seen, but the plastic tub was resting, empty, in her former spot on the sofa. I checked the bathroom—empty too. And then I heard bumps overhead.

I slowly climbed the stairs to the loft, halting when my head just cleared the top step. There she was, pacing carefully, heel to toe, with her hands perched on her hips.

"What are you doing?"

"This is nuts." She didn't even look in my direction. "You have this whole amazing space up here, and you're not using it?"

"I just moved in." My excuse immediately rang as lame in my own ears as it must have sounded to her. The truth was that I'd been intimidated by the loft, as though any attempt I might make to turn it into a habitat would spoil it. It really was that amazing.

Hardwood floors, just like on the main level, but the walls were entirely glass, affording a three-hundred-and-sixty-degree view—basically a glass hut perched atop one of the cargo containers which comprised the main floor. Up here, I could see everything, but everything could also see me, which gave me an uncomfortable case of prickles.

"Hanging curtains," Willow announced. "That's what you need. With a racking system on the ceiling. You could create smaller pods with them based on function. Your bed should go here." She aligned her arms in a sweeping motion like the ground crew who direct arriving aircraft to their designated gates at the terminal.

There was a dead man just a few steps from my front door, and Willow wanted to talk about interior design? Apparently she'd recovered from the trauma of seeing him and nearly touching him. Or she was desperately seeking a distraction from the grisly memory.

"I was thinking maybe an office," I murmured.

Willow fixed me with a scowl. "There's tons of room. You have to sleep up here too. Come on." She pushed past me on the stairs. "I'll show you."

I straggled after her into the bedroom. She was already on her knees, peering at the underside of the bed frame. "Do you have a Phillips screwdriver? It would take just a few minutes to get these legs off."

I knew that, because I'd screwed the legs onto the frame the day before. "Seriously? You want to move furniture right now?"

"Can you think of anything better to do?"

The child was taking over my life. But she had a point.

The bed frame was actually the easy part. We flopped the foam mattress to the side—sheets, duvet, and my pile of feather Euro pillows included—and tackled the gazillion screws holding the thing together. Willow did have one character trait that could easily be plunked on a résumé—she was an incredibly diligent worker when she set her mind to something. She left me panting in her wake.

Once the frame was reassembled upstairs, we took a short break out at the end of the rooftop deck that ran the full length of the loft atop the other adjoined cargo container. The height of the deck afforded us an excellent view back toward land and of the hubbub on the walkway midway there.

For some reason, the quiet and efficient concentration of the official people below, many of whom knelt or squatted at the edge of the walkway—still investigating, probing, measuring, and photographing without having moved the body yet—reminded me of the importance of adult supervision. "Do you need to let your grandmother know where you are? That you're okay? That you—you know—"

"That I'm emotionally scarred?" Willow snorted and propped her elbow on the railing next to me.

"Well, that goes without saying," I fired back. "Just like everybody else. I meant, will she worry about you?"

"Nah. I think she knows."

I followed the direction of Willow's pointing finger to an even bigger cluster of people on shore, packed into the lighted area just outside the door to the marina office. Willow's grandmother's raven-black beehive hairdo stood out from the rest like the bearskin hat of a Buckingham Palace guard.

Bettina's orange bob was in the mix too. The spectators were keeping a surprising distance from the yellow police tape that blocked off the entrance to the south gangplank, but I realized that the evening's newest development might have outstripped Bettina's welcome party as the social occasion of the season. It appeared as though all the marina's residents and then some were on hand for the morbid activities.

The idea turned my stomach. So I punched Willow lightly on the arm. "How are your muscles?"

"Puny. Why?"

"Because the mattress weighs ten times more than the bed frame, and we can't disassemble it."

I might have exaggerated the mattress's weight, but it more than made up for my overestimation with its unwieldiness. We tried folding it like a taco, but it insisted on slumping open. Willow was at the top of the staircase, tugging. I was at the bottom, shoving. But the king-size foam molded around the balusters and sagged between the risers and refused to budge more than an inch at a time.

"Freezing buckets of mothballs," I grunted. I love my bed—I really do—when I'm in it.

Willow was too short of breath to snort, but she gave me an expressive eye-roll down the long length of immovable, gel-bead-infused, therapeutic foam.

"This was your idea," I reminded her and bent to scoop my arms under the bottom edge of the mattress for another heave.

"Ms. Fairchild?" a rich baritone called from the open front door.

Once again, I was caught with my ass in the air. While wearing a party-appropriate frock that fell a little shy of mid-thigh under the best of circumstances. "Just a moment," I answered sweetly. Or not so sweetly—more like wheezily, and quite possibly, grumpily.

"I need to take your statement." He'd come over to the staircase, and was glaring at me through the balusters while my hair hung in my face and I hyperventilated from the strain.

I straightened and returned the glare. "One condition."

His brows arched over a pair of the yummiest warm and inquisitive brown eyes into an expression so annoying it made me want to reach over and snatch the smirk right off his face.

Instead, I clenched my hands into fists, released one fist to point at the mattress, and said, "This. Upstairs. Then I'll talk all you want."

I hate it when men find me amusing. But, to his credit, this stranger who had just waltzed into my house and must be some kind of police officer set his leather-bound folder on my coffee table and joined me on the stairs. He, uh, smelled good—not at all what you'd expect of someone who gets called out at night to investigate dead bodies—and I found it difficult to look him in those luscious eyes, which were rather above mine, I noticed, even though we were now standing on the same step.

"How about if you help from the top?" he said.

I kicked off my ballet flats and performed a horrible crab-like crawl up the mattress, digging my toes in wherever I could, painfully aware of my creeping hemline. Willow reached for my arm and helped pull me the last couple feet until I was squeezed in beside her. She had a look of indecipherable satisfaction on her scrunchy little face but graciously refrained from offering snide comments.

"Ready?" Mr. Brown Eyes asked.

Somehow, he rolled in the edges of the mattress with his long arms, curved the bulky thing into submission, and lifted it patiently, one step at a time, while Willow and I scrabbled backward and upward, guiding and hoisting, but in no way bearing our fair share of the weight.

Once in the loft, it was easier—a straight shot to the prepared bed frame set at a diagonal in the corner.

Willow did a belly-flop onto the mattress the moment it was in place. "Never again," she groaned into the foam. Then she sprang over onto her back and bounced up to a sitting position, her feet dangling off the edge, her youthful energy instantly restored. "The puke's mine."

My mouth fell open, and I blinked at her.

But the strong stranger nodded somberly. "Good to know."

"Coffee." The word came out startlingly clear and a little too loud. They both swiveled to stare at me, but I spun and marched toward the stairs. No reason we couldn't be civilized about this. Besides, I thought it best to get Mr. Brown Eyes out of proximity to my bed as soon as possible. I didn't want him getting any ideas.

I knew I'd end up rearranging my kitchen once I started using it in earnest, but for now all my tools and supplies were tucked neatly into cupboards. I pulled out the French press, a grinder, and a bag of Stumptown coffee beans Sloane had insisted I try. Within minutes, I had a kettle heating water on the stove, cream in a little ceramic pitcher, and brown sugar in my favorite hand blown glass bowl along with napkins and spoons set out on the bar-height counter that separated the kitchen from the living room.

Willow had perched on a stool across the counter and was watching me closely as though she was mentally recording the proper steps to coffee service. Mr. Brown Eyes had retrieved his folder and straddled a stool beside her. He, too, seemed very interested in the coffee-making process. So I hovered near the stove and examined the air just above the kettle spout for any sign of a steam disturbance.

Mr. Brown Eyes cleared his throat, lifted a cheek, pulled a wallet from his back jeans pocket, opened it, and produced a card which he placed face-up on the counter and pushed in my direction. "Detective Vaughn Malloy," he said, even though I could easily read his name on the card from where I was standing. It also said 'Fidelity Police Department' with a couple phone numbers and a snazzy logo in blue ink.

Fidelity was the name of the closest town I'd been trying to remember when I'd dialed 911. In fact, the marina's address was in the Fidelity zip code. I probably should have been able to recall such an honorable moniker, but staring at a dead guy had vaporized all the pertinent details from my mind.

"I'd be happy if you just called me Vaughn," he added.

Willow had a wolfish grin on her face and was making googly eyes at me. No doubt the kid was suffering from low blood sugar given her empty stomach and recent weight-lifting workout. I reached into a cupboard for a package of granola and plunked it in front of her along with a bowl. "Use the cream."

A piercing whistle started, and I jumped to pour the hot water into the French press. When we were all plied with the necessary nourishment, I fixed Vaughn with what I hoped was a steady gaze. "What do you need to know?"

It has to be difficult to talk with people about the dead bodies they've found. Not exactly in the realm of normal social pleasantries. He asked for a time line of the evening's events, which I supplied, augmented by Willow's more colorful remarks. He took copious notes on the letter-size pad in his folder. Big hands, scratchy writing. I couldn't decipher the words upside down.

"You don't have an accent," Vaughn said, catching me off guard. "Didn't you just move here from the East Coast?"

I frowned. My history had nothing to do with the flurry of police activity on the walkway outside. "It was never that pronounced, and four years of college in California cured me completely."

"Huh." His brown eyes narrowed. "You're out here at the end of the A row all by yourself."

It sounded like an accusation.

I shrugged, but didn't give him the benefit of a scowl. "It's where the house was already moored and hooked up to utilities. Easiest to keep it in place rather than relocate it."

"Gran gave her a move-in special on the lease," Willow volunteered, "since she's so low-maintenance."

Her grammar was a little loose. I wasn't sure if she meant that her grandmother was low-maintenance or that I was. But given the amounts of hair spray and eye shadow Roxy Sperry applied daily, I was certain I'd win the low-maintenance contest, if anyone was measuring.

Vaughn was, although I couldn't tell what criteria he was using. But he was definitely sizing me up. Silently.

Well, I can out-silent just about anyone. I bit my lip and lifted the French press in a noiseless offer of more coffee. He accepted by sliding his mug closer.

His dark brown hair, which had a sprinkling of silver mixed in, was just long enough to reveal that his follicles tended to have minds of their own. If he let his hair grow more than a couple inches, it would become a curly mop. Definitely a magnet for a woman's hands.

Carefully trimmed sideburns, crow's-feet creases radiating from the outside corners of his eyes, thick brows, a nose with a little bump on the bridge that looked as though it hadn't been set perfectly after being broken, and maybe a hint of sunburn on his tanned skin. But mostly I was struck by his calmness. I hoped it hadn't come from dealing with this kind of situation on a regular basis, but it probably was the demeanor of an experienced detective.

And that thought prompted a question I couldn't help but ask. "Do you know who he is, the man? I hope his family—" I winced. This was going to be awful for them, no matter what.

I'd been so young that I'd been spared the torment of seeing police officers at the door after my mother had been killed. But I'd known they'd come, sensed their somber presence and quiet voices in the foyer, endured the tension in my nanny's insistent hugs, and absorbed the same hollow, distant pain my father had acquired after he'd rushed home from his business trip.

Vaughn wrapped his long fingers around the mug. "We have a pretty good idea. The ME will have to confirm and notify relatives before we announce it, though."

"Of course," I murmured. But there was something—this death was going to require an announcement. I knew the names of those who died in unusual ways were usually released in short official statements. But announced?

Vaughn's expression let me know that I wouldn't be getting any more information out of him. That amused tilt of his lips again. He knew I was sizing him up, too.

Might as well let the man do his job. I pushed back from the counter and started collecting dirty dishes.

Vaughn drained his mug and handed it to me. "Thanks. Best I've had in a long time." He nodded toward his card still lying on the counter. "Call me if you need anything or remember anything else. I like details. And intuitions. They're usually right."

I couldn't help smiling a little at that. Intuitions. And a man who came right out and said they were valuable. I trailed him to the door.

He turned and angled one of his thick brows at me. "Lock this?" His hand was on the door knob, and even though his statement sounded like a question, it was also a command. "It'll be busy out here for a while."

Willow wedged into the doorway with me, and we watched him walk away.

"I told you he was hunky," she murmured.

It took me a full minute. Mainly because the height difference between mother and son was so extreme. The keen brown eyes, however, bore a striking resemblance.

"Willow," I said in a warning tone, "you promised no collusion."

She gaped up at me. "No way. Bettina might be, uh, pushy—but there's no way she planted that dead guy just so you'd meet Vaughn." She shook her head indignantly. "No way. This is just one of those things. He investigates major crimes, so it makes sense he'd be called out for a dead body." She sniffled. "Sad, really. Can I stay here tonight? I don't want to fight through that"—she pointed toward the knot of people still clogging the walkway and the additional rapid comings and goings along the gangplank—"to get home."

CHAPTER 4

I insisted that Willow call her grandmother. She did so from the roof deck, complete with vigorous waving and jumping jacks while the phone was pressed against her ear to ensure her visibility across the marina. I suspected Detective Malloy had already informed Roxy that her granddaughter was alive and well on the other side of the police tape. From the office, the woman with the giant beehive hairdo raised her hand in acknowledgment of Willow's antics and readily gave permission for a sleepover.

We spent the next hour setting up my new sleeping area in the loft. Willow thoroughly and convincingly explained her vision for curtains that would provide both a modicum of privacy and separation from the rest of the loft, and I agreed to make a run to IKEA in the next few days for the necessary hardware and fabric.

When we'd exhausted that subject, Willow turned her attention to the potential for an office at the other end of the loft. I turned my attention to the clock—nearing midnight. But she was going strong, and she was doggedly avoiding my attempts to discuss our discovery of the dead man.

The experience had to have jolted her—having spewed her stomach contents was proof of that. I just hoped she'd open up at some point and not internalize too much. But I wouldn't pressure her.

So I found myself seated on the floor underneath my desk, speaking on the phone with the technical support department of my internet provider. A few presses of the reset button on the router plus two complete reboots while we listened to each other breathe on opposite ends of the line, and we were in business.

When I crawled out from under the desk, Willow was engrossed in matching up my selection of art supplies with suitable containers. I use old vases, bowls, and baskets to keep everything I need easily at hand, but I'd had to consolidate when I'd packed. Willow was un-consolidating.

"What do you do, exactly?" she asked.

"Good question. Most of this stuff is really just for my hobby—or hobbies, or maybe obsessions—but I'm hoping to turn it into a business."

My answer was not sufficient. Willow flashed me a scrunched sneer that I was learning indicated annoyance. "What did you *used to do*, before you moved?"

Ah—the unemployment problem. I felt like sneering myself. "Truth? It's majorly embarrassing."

"Oh yeah?" Willow stuffed loose strands of blue hair behind her ears with an eager grin.

I sighed. "Yeah. I designed emails."

"Yuck."

"Tell me about it."

"But why is that embarrassing?"

"Because they were copycats."

The non-disclosure agreement I'd signed when I'd been hired had been very specific. And my friend from the human resources department, Kris, had reiterated that all of its minute points still held, pretty much for the rest of my life, even though I was no longer gainfully employed by that particular contractor for the National Security Agency.

And then I thought, *she's a blue-haired kid with a penchant for space opera. And she's just seen what is probably her first dead body. Shoot—it was my first dead body. It's been a rough night. Why not tell her?*

So I amended, "They were perfect copies. Otherwise known as spear phishing. All for a good cause, of course." I choked a bit on the last sentence, because I didn't entirely believe it, at least not in every single instance. But that horrid non-disclosure agreement did still have its hooks in me, at least about some things.

"Whoa. That's vicious." Willow squinted hard as she leaped to the obvious, but inaccurate, conclusion. "You stole money from little old ladies' bank accounts?"

"The targets were mostly—allegedly—terrorist masterminds and financiers. Nobody you'd regard as innocent. And I don't think the people I worked for stole anything once they were in. Just watched. But I can't say for sure, because that part wasn't my responsibility."

"Is this—like—a *secret*?" Willow whispered.

I nodded.

"Whoa," she said again. Then she leaned a hip against my desk and held up an assortment of colored pencils. "How are you going to make a business out of these?"

Hurrah for changing the subject. Willow had more positive social wiles than I'd given her credit for. "Marketing, graphic design, brand strategy, consultant-for-hire, et cetera. Among other things, I'm pretty good at designing logos, and I prefer to start with more tactile media before scanning the artwork over to digital. What do you think?"

Her mouth shifted into a dubious pucker. "Fine," she muttered. "Sure. Knock yourself out."

"Or starve," I added cheerfully.

~oOo~

The next morning, I cranked out the Five Tibetans on the rooftop deck just outside my new sleeping area and immediately saw the wisdom in Willow's interior design scheme. Since I wasn't at water level, there were no nosy neighbors to paddle alongside and interrupt me. No witnesses to my contorted body positions. Well, one—but I was pretty sure the great blue heron winging by with his long neck crooked in on itself didn't give me a second glance. Therefore no embarrassment. And the view was spectacular. A two-for-one deal.

Willow was gone. She'd left the sheets and blankets I had used to turn the sofa into a cozy nest for her folded neatly on the coffee table. No note; no dirty dishes in the sink. And she'd relocked the front door behind her, per Detective Malloy's order.

I unlocked the door and pulled it open. The walkway was deserted. Only a forgotten knot of yellow police tape around a lamppost remained of the previous night's events. If I squeezed my eyes shut and pretended really hard, I might be able to convince myself none of it had actually happened. Almost. Too bad the technique doesn't work.

Instead, my imagination flitted to what the family of the dead man must be going through right now. I wondered if they'd been notified yet. How long had he been missing—a few hours, a few days? Had they been living with a growing sense of dread filling their hearts, waiting for a phone call? Or had he been expected at home any moment, having just run out on a quick errand?

Ugh. Speculation doesn't solve anything. But I was feeling an overwhelming urge to talk about it with someone, and I realized that, the night before, I'd been hoping Willow would want to talk for my benefit as much as for hers. There was no way I would call Detective Malloy with my emotional neediness, even though he'd offered that unqualified *anything* as a reason to call. Sloane and her family were at church this morning, so my best sounding board was unavailable at the moment too.

That left one option. I pulled my hair into a ponytail and snugged the laces on my cross-trainers.

A wildlife refuge abutted the south end of the marina, the next property upriver from where my house floated in the A-17 slip. It was probably home to the great blue heron who'd been commuting overhead. On the map, the refuge was a long, skinny green strip that occupied the space between the river and the county road which was several hundred yards inland and paralleled the water.

According to the brochure I'd seen in the marina office, the refuge served as a rest stop for migratory birds as well as provided nesting habitat for year-rounders. While there were undeveloped trails and limited public access, the refuge's main purpose was to serve wildlife, not humans. In other words, don't expect flush toilets and picnic tables. And if a bear or cougar wanted to eat you while you were in the refuge, well, good luck with that. Which was fine with me.

But I also grabbed my pepper spray canister and stuffed it in my pocket, just in case.

I found a feeble hint of a hard-packed trail amid the mounding blackberries that marked the edge of the marina's parking lot. Scooting through sideways to avoid the thorns, I was quickly overshadowed by a loose, volunteer forest of cottonwoods and poplars intermixed with a few coniferous trees, maybe pines? I added a tree identification book to my growing mental list of field guides I would need to fully appreciate my new home.

I'm not a runner; not even a jogger. But all those lunchtime power walks with my friend Kris had served me well in the stamina department. Besides, I wanted to catch glimpses of the wildlife, not scare the creatures away with manically pumping legs and flailing arms.

The path widened. Dotted with half-buried rocks, zigzagged by tree roots, requiring constant vigilance so I didn't end up in a face-plant with a nasty twisted ankle, but, oh, so worth it. Chirpy little birds swarmed the leafy canopy—flitting, rustling, and not at all disturbed by my presence.

Scattered crackling in the underbrush made me jump a few times, but whatever creatures were making those noises didn't want me to see them. I took a measure of comfort from the fact that they were shier than I was. As long as none of them turned out to be snakes or skunks, everything would be just fine.

The path wound toward the river and eventually emerged into a more open area along a sandy beach. Well, partly sand and partly mud—the high tide line was clearly etched into the riverbank that was cut away above the beach. Apparently I'd timed my early morning foray with low tide. During her introductory spiel for new lessees, Roxy had warned me that the Pacific Ocean tides affect the Columbia and Willamette rivers—and thus my house— even though the marina was roughly sixty miles from the coast and even farther if measured in squiggly river miles.

The water lapped the sand in gentle swells, and a bird with long, shockingly bright yellow legs high-stepped its way along the shore. I froze, not wanting to interrupt the bird if it was foraging for breakfast. Its peculiar gait was both comical and endearing.

And then there was a noise that shouldn't have been in that peaceful spot—rough male laughter.

The kind of sound that makes a woman cringe and sets off the inner claxon alarm of her self-protection radar. I don't think guys understand this—the automatic, involuntary response we have to certain of their behaviors, but I also suspect that this response has saved many women's lives, provided they paid attention to it.

The bird didn't like the raucous disturbance either. It took off running, neck outstretched, and launched into flight.

There were three of them, just coming into view around the bend. They were joking and jostling each other while one of them pushed what appeared to be a slender unicycle ahead of him. He paused to jot notes on a clipboard. I bent low and scurried—subtly, I hoped— toward the muddy bank and the safety of the trees beyond.

The urgency I felt was irrational—should have been irrational. But the frantic niggle was still there, prodding at the back of my brain. At that moment, I would have much rather encountered a bear than one of those men, let alone all three men together.

I slid a few times on the mud before gaining purchase, then I was up and over and crouching in some accommodating ferns. I snuck a quick look down at my clothing. Gray hoodie and darker gray capri yoga leggings—good for blending in. My cross-trainers, however, were neon lime green. Then again, I was in a forest with a lot of other greens.

But curiosity held me in place as the men moved closer. These guys weren't nature lovers or outdoorsy athletes—the kind you would reasonably expect to encounter on an early Sunday morning in a wildlife refuge.

They were dressed in khakis and loafers, button-down shirts with the long sleeves rolled up to their elbows. Casual clothes, but not walk-on-the-beach clothes. More telling because they hadn't removed their shoes to go barefoot.

The laughter was getting louder and coarser, ricocheting off the mud flats and tree trunks. A minute later, I saw the reason why. A shiny silver flask removed from a pocket and passed around. The owner of the flask sipped both first and last—effectively doubling up on his buddies—before returning it to his pocket.

And the unicycle-looking thing turned out to be a measuring wheel. There were frequent pauses in their leisurely stroll while the man with the clipboard recorded information. He seemed more serious and focused than his two companions, but, altogether, they appeared to be celebrating something.

When they'd passed me, I stood and stretched my cramped legs. My arm brushed against the hard lump of the pepper spray canister in my pocket, and the silliness of my position flooded over me. Hiding like a scaredy-cat. I had as much right to be on that beach as they did. Me and my hyperactive amygdala.

I turned and retraced my steps toward home.

When I reached the marina, the office was open, where I found Roxy engaged in the ritual of lighting up another cigarette. The flick of the lighter, the cigarette pressed to her lips while clamped between the first and second fingers of her left hand, the hollow sucking of her cheeks as she inhaled, the flaring glow at the end of the cigarette; then the simultaneous removal of the cigarette from her mouth, the thump of the lighter in her right hand on the counter, and an exhale of swirly blue-gray smoke into the already dense atmosphere accompanied by a satisfied sound deep in her throat.

I'd been privy to that particular sequence of actions a dozen or more times over the course of the two hours it had taken to sign the moorage lease and be indoctrinated with all the guidelines and regulations of the marina's homeowners' association. She wasn't exactly a chain-smoker, but only because she chose to ignite each new cigarette with a lighter rather than the butt of the previous one.

Our orientation session had also given me the opportunity to memorize the definition of *gadfly* because it was the featured (two days past date) term on her word-a-day calendar. I'd been sorely tempted to reach over and tear the sheet off, but had heroically restrained myself. Because I refuse—or at least try really hard—*not* to be a gadfly. Today's word was *esoteric*, and I decided to ignore it.

I suspected Roxy was walking a very fine line in that shady area next to the laws about not smoking in public places or in places of business. Only the fact that the marina office was tacked onto the front of her apartment—the private, on-site residence provided for the marina manager—made such unhealthy crossover possible.

My eyes were already watering from the sting of secondhand smoke, but there was something I had to do. "Did you see Willow this morning?" I asked.

Roxy grunted. "Drove her to that sci-fi writing group she goes to. Every Sunday they hang out in hoity-toity coffee shops in Portland and *brainstorm*." She scooped her fingers—and cigarette—in the air to encase the last word in aerial quotation marks.

I grinned. "She's a smart kid."

Roxy exhaled and pressed the heels of her hands on the counter. She tilted her head—along with the entire shellacked hair sculpture on top of it—while studying me with a contemplative look. "Yeah. I guess she is." Another drag on the cigarette. "All I know is she keeps me organized."

I nodded. "I was the beneficiary of that particular skill set last night. You should see my desk. Anyway, I wanted to check with you about the cooking lessons. Did she tell you about that?"

Again, Roxy's black eyes settled on me, not rudely, but as though she was trying to penetrate through my outer layers. Then she shrugged. "Looks like you got yourself a shadow. But if she's ever any trouble, or an annoyance, just let me know. I'll put a stop to it."

I wasn't quite sure how to respond. So I nodded again and turned to leave.

"Willow says you're looking for work," Roxy said behind me.

I turned back.

She stabbed at a pile of junk mailers on the counter with her cigarette. The phony smile of a middle-aged white man with red check marks poised in boxes beside his head graced the top flier. "It's election season. We have some biggies coming up in the state legislature and the scrabble for city of Portland positions is as contentious as it ever is—which is to say, a lot. The mudslinging's already clogging the news, and it's only September. If anybody ever needed a brand image improvement, it's politicians. I know it's the bottom of the barrel as far as decent work goes, but I figured you'd have to start somewhere." She shrugged. "Anyway, it's an idea."

"Thank you," I managed. Actually, she was right. In my experience, desperate wanna-be politicians do tend to fling money around in an attempt to ease their pain, or inflict it on others.

I had one foot over the threshold when Roxy's voice halted me once more. "Heard you met our Vaughn last night."

I turned and cocked my head. I probably squinted too. "Your Vaughn?"

"Bettina's Vaughn," Roxy amended. "But everybody around here's been so involved in—or at least aware of—her attempts to set up the poor boy that it feels like he belongs to all of us."

"Ah."

"At one time, I thought he'd do for my daughter, Jody—Willow's mother—but, well"—she flicked ashes into the wobbly half clamshell that served as her ashtray—"not exactly in the same bailiwick, those two, at least not now."

"You're not going to..." I stuttered to a stop.

Roxy cackled at my dismay. "Nope. Adults. Both of you. You'll make your own decisions. But good luck."

The merriment in those dark eyes made me chuckle too. I might actually like this woman.

CHAPTER 5

Speaking of the rather hunky son of a desperate woman and the subject of so much speculation among the marina residents, he was standing on the A walkway—directly between me and my house. But he wasn't alone.

Closer to shore, a young couple was kneeling on the weather-beaten planks near a mound of flower bouquets in cellophane wrappers and homemade signs. Several Mylar balloons floated above the display, their ribbon ties anchored to the walkway. While I stared in shock, the young man flicked a lighter and lit a votive candle in a glass holder.

Then they rose and shuffled past me, toward the gangplank. The girl was sniffling, and he wrapped an arm around her tightly, pulling her head into his shoulder.

All the warnings about fire that Roxy had pounded into me during my orientation screeched through my head. I had thought it ironic at the time, the warnings coming from a near chain-smoker, but I understood the threat. Open fire and boats, including floating houses, are never, ever a good combination. Since the marina office was on dry land, safely ensconced at the edge of the gravel parking lot, Roxy's position on the subject wasn't hypocritical, and was, in fact, required by the marina's insurance company.

I cast a quick glance over my shoulder to make sure the young couple wouldn't notice, then I pounced forward and extinguished the flame.

"What is going on?" I muttered. People lighting fires on the walkway to my house? Of all the inane, irresponsible, selfish—

"I'll take care of it." Vaughn must have heard my not-too-quiet complaint. His footsteps resounded on the walkway, and he joined me at the makeshift memorial at the A-7 slip.

Because that's what it was—the flowers, balloons, and farewell messages. *RIP Ian. We love you. You'll be missed forever, Ian. Happy trails.* The notes were scrawled on torn pieces of cardboard and poster board. Some of them were crowded with signatures. Ian had been a popular guy.

"But"—I glanced around and then pointed to the spot were Vaughn had been standing the moment before—"I thought—wasn't he over there in slip A-11? I mean, it was dark, but I'm pretty sure..."

"Yep. But they don't know that," Vaughn replied. There was a smile in his voice. "You have a good memory."

I squinted up at him. Up! How long had it been since I'd looked up at anyone? Well, except since last night? The observation re-stunned me for a moment. "I thought—you said—" My words got stuck on each other. "Um, have you made the announcement yet? How do they know? I mean, about *here*? And who?"

Vaughn sighed. "We haven't made the announcement yet because the ME's still working on notifying relatives. But Mr. Thorpe had been missing for several days. People were on edge, waiting for news. It's a situation where, once there are rumors, they travel like wildfire." A little smirk lightened his brown eyes.

I scowled. "Yeah, wildfire right up this wooden walkway to my house."

"I'll take care of it," Vaughn repeated. "I'll talk to Roxy about posting No Trespassing signs in the parking lot. If she does that, then we can station a uniformed officer up there to enforce a perimeter. People will still want—and need—to establish a memorial, but we'll get them to do it in a safer place."

"Okay." I felt incredibly callous. Of course the dead man's friends would be grieving and need a way to express their feelings. "Thank you." It came out as an afterthought, but I meant it. I peered up at Vaughn again, but he was staring at my legs.

"You're bleeding."

"What? Oh." A quick glance down revealed a couple scratches on my right shin that had dribbled blood in thin trails down to my ankle and into my sock. Not to mention all the mud smeared on my clothing. The result of scrabbling up a riverbank in a hurry. "I'm fine." I waved off the minor injuries with an attempt at nonchalance.

Vaughn wasn't buying it. At all. Those brown eyes turned starkly serious. "Was this your first dead body?"

"Yes. Well, no. I mean yes, that I've seen. My mother died when I was young, but it was closed-casket, the funeral, because she crashed into a tree, so I never saw...um, yes." I closed my eyes and just stood there in the warm sunshine, swaying slightly with the walkway's rocking motion. Why was I suddenly a blithering idiot?

"I thought so," Vaughn said gently. His fingertips brushed my arm. "The urge to rearrange heavy furniture, impeccable hospitality and amazing coffee at a moment's notice...and wallowing in mud." His eyes examined me from shoulders to cross-trainers and back up again, finally settling on my face. "Yeah, you're exhibiting all the classic signs of shock." There it was again—the way the corners of his lips barely turned up.

I couldn't keep from bursting out laughing. Maybe it was from relief that my inexplicable emotional spasms—which I'd thought I'd kept pretty well internalized—might be normal. "If you say so."

Roxy hadn't said a word about my disheveled appearance. But on the whole, I rather thought Roxy was adept at selectively *not* mentioning things. That whole dialogue in the office, and we'd never once alluded to the dead man, either. I wondered how Willow dealt with those gaping holes in communication, or if it was normal to her, one of the consequences of a broken home to which I could relate.

"Why are you here?" I blurted rather rudely. Not that I was complaining, actually, but... "Isn't the police work here finished?"

"It's good to look at a scene in daylight. Fresh perspective." Vaughn's face was angled upriver toward the few boats that were bobbing on the water, already anchored in place for a day of leisure.

"How far did he—I mean, where do you think he fell in?" I asked. "Was he in the water the whole time he was missing? Did he know how to swim?" My stomach clenched in a fitful contraction just thinking about my little nieces who'd delighted in the novel experience of trotting back and forth on the floating walkway. While they'd been wearing life jackets and had always been within sight of several adults, the prospect of one of them falling into the water sent a shiver through me. I was going to be even more hyper-vigilant whenever they came to visit.

"The ME will give us an estimate of how long Ian was in the water after he's done the autopsy. Drowning time of death can be hard to pinpoint because so much has to do with the temperature of the water and how submerged the body was and whether or not it encountered underwater obstacles. Ian was last seen Tuesday night at a meeting of the Friends of River Otters group where he was a featured speaker. He lingered for a while afterward to talk with people, then left on foot, presumably walked to his apartment a few blocks away, but we haven't been able to confirm that. The clothes he was wearing last night, however, were not the same clothes he wore at that meeting."

I thought that maybe Vaughn was trying to distract me with technical details, to make the idea of a dead body more factual and less personal. But he'd also called the man by his first name this time. "Did you know him?" I asked.

The small fraction of a smile was back. "I arrested him a few times. And donated to a couple of his causes too. Ian was"—Vaughn shook his head—"enigmatic. A real character."

How does a police detective grieve? I touched his arm. "I'm sorry."

Vaughn gazed at me for a long minute, his brown eyes thoughtful but also a little distant. His mind was clearly elsewhere. Finally, he inhaled deeply, breaking off the reverie. "I should go. Paperwork calls. See you around, Ms. Fairchild." He stepped past me and continued on toward the gangplank with a long, unhurried stride.

~oOo~

Google. It's an amazing service. It enables unprecedented degrees of busybody behavior, and better yet, nobody (other than the NSA and maybe the GCHQ—oh, and the advertisers who buy the aggregated search data which may or may not be personally identifying) even knows you were spying on your friends and neighbors and other people wholly unknown to you. People like Ian Thorpe, for example.

I showered in record time and made a beeline for my new, thoroughly organized, and immaculate office in the loft. I couldn't account for my curiosity. Except that maybe it was because Willow and I had found him. Or maybe—and I thought this was perhaps even more the case—it was because of Vaughn's reaction to his death. I wouldn't call Vaughn's response moodiness exactly. Definitely not the grouchiness Bettina had mentioned. But there was something bothering him. So it bothered me too—whatever it was.

Ian Thorpe's name popped up all over the place—a whole slew of articles on the major local news websites plus a few on national news sites. He was on the board of at least eight environmental nonprofit organizations—only one of which, however, had already posted a sorrowful notification about Ian's death on their home page. It appeared the rest of the organizations were following the proper protocol of waiting until after the official police announcement.

I arranged the news articles in chronological order and started reading. Ian was 49 years old. From his early twenties he'd been a frequent and ardent environmental activist. He'd done everything from camping two hundred feet up in a Northern California redwood to keep it from being chopped down to suspending himself from the St. John's bridge to prevent an icebreaker ship that had been in a Portland dry dock for repairs from heading to the Arctic for an oil-drilling operation. Consequently, along with a plethora of friends and supporters, he'd also developed a long list of powerful S&P 500-indexed corporations that hated his guts.

I did a few tangential searches on the names of the public information officers for these corporations who were quoted in the articles. They provided an interesting maze of employment cross-pollination as many of the spokespersons had switched jobs, jumping from subsidiary to subsidiary of related companies—most of which were in the oil-and-gas and mineral exploration sectors. Those businesses run some of the most secretive ventures on the planet, and Ian Thorpe had been determined to reveal their intentions to anybody and everybody. There would be several executives in three-piece suits who would be figuratively dancing at Ian's funeral.

There were no mentions in the local news of Ian's disappearance, no appeals to the public to help locate him. Based on the earlier articles about his activism, I assumed Ian had been fiercely independent and self-sufficient, which was probably why an organized search and rescue operation hadn't yet been launched. Why waste public resources looking for a man who is known to be able to take care of himself?

I'd forgotten to ask Vaughn about Ian's family, but none of the news articles had mentioned a wife or children, so maybe there hadn't been anybody at home to miss him immediately, to know that his schedule had been disrupted. Yet someone had reported him missing—maybe a friend or fellow activist.

Apparently, the times when Vaughn had arrested Ian also hadn't been newsworthy. I suspected the incidents had been for local protests that had turned into public nuisances or had blocked private property—and that what happened in Fidelity stayed in Fidelity because it was such a small town. Or maybe the arrests were for more personal reasons like DUI or shoplifting or something. Which was none of my business. Absolutely not.

Disgusted with my voyeurism, I turned to home improvement websites. After two full days of residence in the house, I'd realized that, while the whole place was shabby, the exterior was the worst. With winter coming, it had to be my priority. I needed to find a place where I could rent a pressure washer and then an electric paint sprayer. And I would need to pick paint colors. So many decisions.

I moved out to the rooftop deck with my laptop and a pile of pillows for comfortable seating—proper patio furniture would have to wait until I figured out how much the exterior improvements would cost—to enjoy the sunshine and the increased activity on the river.

Speedboats towing water skiers in wet suits; sailboats tacking back and forth with taut white sails straining against the rigging; men wearing brightly colored life jackets and zipping around on all sorts of personal watercraft trying to impress the women in bikinis who were sunbathing on the decks of anchored yachts; and lowly kayakers near the shores, dipping their paddles in the sparkling water.

The wakes from all the passing boats set my house to a gentle sloshing that I found mesmerizing—and so relaxing that my eyes may have closed for a few minutes. It was like being rocked in a cradle. Of course, the motion was accompanied by buzzing outboard motor noises and the creak and clank of the floating walkway adjusting to the water movement. But it was all remarkably peaceful.

"Hey, Eva!" hollered a now familiar voice.

I cracked open one eye and squinted through the deck railing.

My favorite blue-haired kid waved frantically, as though I might somehow accidentally overlook her standing down below, just outside my front door.

"Didn't you hear me knocking?" she shouted.

I trotted downstairs so we could converse at a more civilized volume.

"I have great news," she announced, squeezing past me when I opened the door and leading the way back up the stairs.

"Come on in," I muttered.

Willow rearranged the pillows and proceeded to make herself quite comfortable. She sat cross-legged with her hands clasped in front of her, her gray eyes wide with anticipation. "Guess what?"

I wasn't in the mood for a quiz-show method of relaying information. "You're going to have to tell me."

She whipped a small card out of her back pocket and thrust it at me. "Darren wants you to call him."

"Whoa." I held out my hands, palms flat against Willow's presumptuousness. "I thought I'd already made it abundantly clear that I do not need a boyfriend."

"No, silly. For a job. He owns Wicked Bean in the Pearl District where my writing group meets sometimes. He needs a graphic designer to develop promotional stuff for the new section of his shop—a sort of collective creative work space with evening art showcases and gallery exhibits. I told him all about you and he's super excited."

"Right," I groused, accepting the business card. Someone, presumably Darren Hunt, whose name and business information were printed on the front of the card, had also scrawled a couple more phone numbers and an additional email address on the back along with a *Talk soon!* message.

"He said the space will be ready to open next week and he needs it to start paying for itself, but he's terrible at marketing," Willow continued. "Didn't I do good? I got you your first job." She was bouncing on the pillows now, her face alight with pleasure.

I cracked a grin at her. "So maybe I owe you dinner. But seriously, Wicked Bean?"

Willow laughed delightedly, rocking backward with her arms clasped around her knees to collapse on the pillows. Her response came out a little muffled. "I know. Awesome, right? It's one of my favorite coffee shops. And Darren's soooo nice."

Ah. Now the picture was coming together. Darren just might be the object of a teenage crush. "Well, I guess I can talk to the guy. And I need to put together a portfolio—something I haven't done since college."

"Can I help?" Willow popped back up, her hair sticking out at static-y angles.

"Nope. It has to be my own work, examples of what I could offer potential clients. However, you can help me pick a paint color for the house." I held up a warning finger. "Something neutral."

~oOo~

"What am I supposed to do with this?" Willow balanced the onion on her open palm.

"Chop." I pointed to the knife and cutting board I'd laid on the counter for her use.

"How?" She must have seen the look on my face, because she added. "When I said Gran and I eat stuff only from cans and boxes, I meant it." She picked at the onion's dry root fringe and wrinkled her nose. "What is this? I don't think I want to eat it."

I chuckled. "It grew in the ground, and it has its own protective covering—a *package*, if you will. We're going to throw away the skin." I retrieved the poor, maligned bulb and demonstrated the proper technique for separating the edible from the inedible parts. And thus, Willow gained her first experience of weeping over an onion.

I also got to be the one who informed her that bacon doesn't just *come from* pigs, it *is* pig. That, and other startling revelations during the course of our meal preparation, seemed to completely distort Willow's previous worldview. But we ended up producing a delicious Denver omelet, a large portion of which she polished off without any apparent qualms.

A resounding knock on the front door came as Willow pulled the plug in the sink, releasing the soapy water. I'd made her hand-wash all the dishes so she would learn how much of a commitment good food required. But the extra work hadn't seemed to deter her in the least.

Bettina stood outside, clutching my bowl against her middle. Her outfit du jour was a sparkly turquoise number—wide-legged, mid-calf culottes topped by a tunic that was embroidered at the neck. The ensemble certainly set off her orange hair. Once again, she was dripping with jewelry, this time of an abalone and silver persuasion.

I stepped aside with a wide smile. "Come in."

But Bettina peered inside, spotted Willow busily drying dishes and returning them to their spots in the cupboards, and frowned. "I don't want to intrude."

Oh really? I didn't believe it for a second, but she did have a forlorn air about her today, not the exuberant bossiness she'd exhibited earlier.

"We're just finishing up," I said, "but you're in time for coffee."

"And I've gotta go." Willow appeared at my elbow and gave me a conspiratorial wink. "I'm supposed to be doing homework—or something." She dodged through the congestion in the doorway and called over her shoulder once she reached the walkway, "Besides, I can take a hint."

"That girl," Bettina muttered, but she stepped inside and gazed around at the improvements.

I eased the bowl out of her grasp and repeated, "Coffee?"

"No, no." Bettina waved dismissively, sending her bracelets clinking. "I'm not going to stay."

And yet, there she stood in the middle of my living room.

"Okay." I retreated to the kitchen and began the preparations for coffee regardless.

Bettina sidled up to the bar and hoisted herself onto a stool. I smiled over the grinder. It appeared as though I was in for a repeat of the previous night, except with Vaughn's mother in attendance instead of the detective himself.

"I understand if he's not your type," Bettina said.

Uh-oh. I needed to take her firmly in hand before the situation got out of control. I turned and propped a fist on my hip as I stared at her. "I've had a total of two interactions with your son in the past two days. They were both of a professional nature, as I'm sure you're aware."

Bettina nodded solemnly. "Story of my life."

I scowled but kept talking. I wasn't going to let her derail my perfectly logical presentation. "Vaughn seems like a reasonable, well-spoken, and thoroughly capable man. Why don't you let him find a girlfriend by himself? I'd be willing to bet—a lot—that you'd both be happier with the results if you did."

Bettina sniffed. "I know," she whispered.

Just like that? She'd capitulated—if her response was sincere—far more easily than I'd expected. I gave her a knowing glare. "But?"

"But nothing." She shrugged. "I'm projecting. I always do. It's a mother's prerogative."

My instant suspicion was a wild leap, but I decided to go for it. Bettina didn't strike me as a woman who needed to be coddled. "Did you just get dumped?" I asked.

"Yy-ess." The admission came out as a tearful whine. Bettina buried her face in her hands.

I dashed to the bathroom for a box of tissues.

CHAPTER 6

"Where's Petula?" I demanded. Because, you know, that's what best friends are for—emotional support. At two-days' acquaintance, I hardly qualified for the position Bettina was putting me in.

"I can't talk to her about this. She warned me about Nigel months ago." Bettina blew her nose—hard—and reached for another tissue.

In spirit, I rolled my eyes. In reality, I slid a mug of coffee in front of her. I wished I had the excuse of homework. I did actually—I needed to get a portfolio in order pronto.

I sighed. Of course, I'd let the woman who'd thrown me a welcome party unburden her soul first.

I knew Nigel was a reprobate the moment Bettina started extolling his virtues. But it was also clear that the poor little orange-haired creature perched on my barstool was desperately lonely. I eventually talked her around to the point that she agreed to write Nigel off as a complete loss.

"And you need to tell everyone so they can hold you to it," I warned. "No relenting. Because you know that creep will come sniveling back, and you'll have to be strong."

Bettina chuckled softly at my words—the first sign of healing.

"In fact"—I was struck by the brilliance of this new idea—"you especially need to tell Vaughn. I'm sure he worries about you." I thought it might be something mother and son could bond over.

"Oh, no." Bettina recoiled visibly and shoved her mug away. "No. Vaughn doesn't need to know. No. No. No." The orange hair swung around her head with her adamancy. "I don't like Vaughn to know I'm dating." She lunged forward and grabbed my hand. "You can't tell him. Please." Her brown eyes were like lasers.

"Uh," I spluttered. "But surely he must know. Your last names aren't the same, so at some point you must have..."

"Remarried. Yes. Once. Very briefly." Bettina released my hand. "After Vaughn left home. It was disastrous. And Vaughn had to deal with—with the aftermath. Because I ended up in the hospital. Bert—well, he hit me. I thought maybe Vaughn would kill him for it."

I stood there blinking, suffering a radical perspective shift myself. Finally, I said, "So he became a police officer."

"Vaughn?" Bettina nodded slowly. "Yes. Like his father. I wasn't excited about that either, but since when has that boy done what I've wanted him to?" A little smile took the bitterness out of her words. It was that same tilting at the corner of her lips—something else Vaughn had inherited from his mother.

"Tell me about Vaughn's father," I said gently.

"Arthur. Arthur Malloy." Bettina's gaze drifted, and I got a glimpse, under the wrinkles and precise makeup, of what she must have been like as a dreamy young girl. "Good Lord, I loved that man. Seven years we were married. Never got an itch he couldn't scratch." She chuckled, but then quickly sobered. "But he must have. Gotten an itch, I mean—an inner torment. He was killed on the side of a county road. He'd gotten out of his cruiser and had some kind of malfunction with his gun. It went off."

Now there was a hollowness to those brown eyes. Bettina reached out and clutched my hand again. "The official cause of death was accident. But I think he committed suicide. His partner, who'd had to testify in court that day—so he wasn't with Arthur when it happened—Chuck Bucknam, he thought so too. But police officers' lives are hard enough without suggesting one of their own couldn't handle the strain. They worry about stuff like that turning epidemic, you know. So we didn't bring it up, just let the investigators go with the accident theory."

I tightened my fingers around her tiny hand. I really wanted to go around the counter and pull her into a hug, but two-days' acquaintance and all those pesky inhibitions...

"Does Vaughn know?" I asked.

Bettina nodded. "He was six years old when it happened, old enough to remember a lot about it. He came to me when he was in his early teens with the hard questions. He brought the newspaper clippings, had gotten ahold of the police report somehow, wanted to know about the gaps in the story that seemed even more obvious with the passage of time." She dabbed at her eyes with a tissue. "That's when I forbade him from ever becoming a police officer himself. Lot of good that did."

"And that's why you worry about him so much." This time I did make the trip around the bar. I wrapped an arm around her and settled onto a stool next to her. "I guess you're allowed a little interference now and then. But"—I gripped her shoulders and turned her to face me at arm's length—"that creep, Nigel, he's toast. Absolute toast, never to be resurrected. Repeat after me."

And I got her to raise her right hand and solemnly swear that Nigel would never be a smudge in her life again. By the end of the cobbled-together oath, Bettina was chuckling, her earrings jangling with the movement.

My most pressing task accomplished, I stretched across the counter and poured the coffee dregs into my mug. "I have a tentative job interview tomorrow and a lot of prep to do tonight—"

"What are you wearing?" Bettina's tone was sharp, and she squinted at me. "Not a suit?"

"Uh, well, I hadn't really gotten that far yet. It's at a coffee shop—"

"Take these." Bettina slid the bangles off her arms, and they clattered on the countertop. "You just got here from the East Coast, so you don't know what it's like, but I can assure you that wearing a suit would be the kiss of death. You need to look artsy, put-together but casual at the same time, like you don't care if you get the job or not."

"But—"

"Shush. I know what I'm talking about. I make jewelry, you know, so I have plenty more where those came from. Now"—she hopped off the stool and pulled me to standing so she could look me up and down—"you should wear a skirt to show off those legs of yours, tights, a pair of boots—mid-calf, I think—a jacket that nips in at the waist, *not* a matching jacket, mind you, and a scarf in a loose twist around your neck, and put your hair up in a messy bun. Do you have glasses? No. That's too bad..." Bettina crossed one arm over her middle and cupped her chin in her other palm. "Glasses make women look smarter. I guess you'll just have to wing it." She held up a finger, accompanied by a broad smile as an idea hit. "I have a pair of readers you could borrow."

Magnifying glasses? "No!" I blurted. I had to draw the line somewhere, and with the way Bettina could rattle on at warp speed, I was already terrifically late. "No," I said more calmly this time. "But thank you. I certainly appreciate the wardrobe advice, and the culture tutorial, but it's time for us to part ways."

Bettina resisted a little, but I managed to usher her to the front door without making it appear like a full-on tug-of-war. I am an awful lot bigger than she is.

"Good night," I said.

Bettina sniffed. "You're right about Nigel. I just needed someone to point out the obvious."

I nodded encouragingly. The more she thought the break-up was her idea, the better.

"Norman's nice. He tells the funniest jokes," Bettina said brightly.

I scowled. "Who's Norman?"

"My Facebook friend. And handsome too." Bettina flittered her fingers at me—silently, since she was sans bangles—and turned on her heel. "And a financial planner," she called over her shoulder as her retreating footsteps thumped on the walkway. "The steady, reliable sort."

~oOo~

On Monday morning, I forced myself to wear one, and one only, of Bettina's bangles, just so I could honestly tell her that I'd made use of her jewelry loan. More than one, and I would end up sounding like a tin peddler while presenting my portfolio—not exactly a stellar professional impression. However, I did take her advice about clothing, particularly the tights and boots since the scabs on my shin were unsightly and would probably prompt comments if I left them exposed.

Darren was amenable to an early morning meeting. I figured a man who owned a coffee shop probably rose before dawn, and he'd sounded chipper enough on the phone that I also assumed he used his product.

I found the Wicked Bean in an old brick warehouse that had been lovingly restored and sectioned into retail businesses. The atmosphere on the whole block was invigorating in a way that extended far beyond the luscious scent of fresh roasted coffee beans. It appeared that the Pearl District benefited from an abundance of foot traffic.

A man with dense, multi-colored tattoos that started at both of his wrists and continued up his arms until they were hidden by the rolled up sleeves of his flannel shirt smiled at me from behind the counter. "You've gotta be Eva." He nodded toward my heavy tote bag and the portfolio clutched under my arm. "What's your poison? It's on the house."

Well, if he was offering... I grinned back and said, "Café bombón."

"Nice. Snag that empty table, will you? I'll be over in a second."

And he was, with a tiny clear glass cup balanced on a saucer. Inside the cup was a beautiful layer of sweetened condensed milk topped by a shot of espresso. "Where'd you develop the habit?" he asked. "Spain?"

"Malaysia. Thank you."

"Really?" His brows pitched up as he slid into the chair opposite me. "And now you're in Portland. Willow raved about you, by the way." He stretched his right hand across the table. "Darren." His fingernails were clipped very short, and they were perfectly clean.

I shook his hand, a smile still stuck on my face. I already liked this guy, and the crazy reason might just be that he seemed to take Willow seriously. How had that suddenly become the criteria by which I judged people?

"I'm rusty," I said. Might as well get the gaping, I-can't-talk-about-it hole in my work history out in the open. "It's been a while since I've consulted with small businesses for a living, but I'll work hard."

"Let's see." Darren gestured for the portfolio, and I handed it to him. I let him page through it without offering commentary. In my experience, trying to explain the subtle meanings and movement embedded in graphic designs is counterproductive. It's better to let people draw their own conclusions, because if the designs aren't perfectly communicative all on their own, they aren't any good anyway.

Darren returned the folder and shoved his chair back. "Did Willow tell you my grand plans?"

"Some."

He tipped his head. "But you'd like to see it in person."

"Yes, I would." I followed him to a locked door in the side wall. He held it open just far enough for me to sidle through with my gigantic bag then locked it behind us. The darkness echoed, and I could tell the room was huge even before Darren found the light switches and flicked them on.

"Wow," I breathed. I didn't know what purpose the cavernous space had served back in the building's warehouse days, but now there was a deep wraparound balcony halfway up the high walls. At two corners, sturdy staircases built out of gleaming mahogany-colored wood rose to the balcony. The contrast between the brick walls and all the polished wood in the balcony railings and staircases was gorgeous. The wall on the street side appeared to be all windows which had been papered over temporarily during the renovations.

"I'm going to install movable dividers on the balcony level and rent out the studio space to craftspeople—writers, painters, textile artists, whatever. Customers are always telling me they're more productive when they work here in the coffee shop than when they try to work at home. I think it has something to do with the ambient noise and the accountability of being visible, so I figured why not extend that and make space for creating permanently available. As it is now, my regulars sort of fight over tables."

I cast a sidelong glance at Darren. His tone of voice had changed as he'd described his vision. He was proud of this space, and he had every reason to be. I was already a bit envious of his tenants, although I wasn't sure, personally, if I could handle the potential noise level. But he was right. Some personalities thrived on having a buzz of activity around them.

"Down here on the main floor, I'll move in more café tables as an annex to the coffee shop," Darren continued. "And in the evenings, I hope to host poetry readings, gallery showings, maybe offer display space for the artists who are tenants. I've applied for a liquor license so I can serve local wines and microbrews during events."

"This is amazing. Can I take pictures?" I asked.

"Be my guest."

I gingerly set my tote bag on the floor and rummaged through it until I found my camera. I attached the 50mm lens first because I wanted texture shots to use as backgrounds. Developing a website and an exclusive community brand for this space would be a cinch. I thought Darren would have a waiting list for studios from the moment he opened the doors and said as much.

"So you'll do it?" he asked.

I turned around and frowned at him. "Don't you want to hear my sales pitch?"

He chuckled. "Nope. I knew you were the right one for the job the moment I saw you, looking all serious with that big bag on your shoulder. If you can schlep that thing around, you'll do fine. But it's a rush."

I spoke from behind the camera as I snapped away. "Your grand opening is this weekend—for the main floor, right? You're going to have questions about the balcony from the get-go. Might as well be ready to answer them. If you have your rental rates set, I could include a rate sheet in the packet. How about if I get sample mock-ups to you Wednesday? That'll give you a day to decide which designs you like. I'll find a printer who'll work on short notice so you'll have some swag for Friday. Do you have any acts lined up for the weekend, any headliners?"

Darren didn't answer right away, so I turned around to check if he was still there.

Hands still wedged in his pockets, he was staring at me with an odd expression on his face. He shook his head with a wry grin. "You take my breath away. I thought *I* was high on caffeine. I could probably rustle up a few poets of the crippling angst and extraterrestrial life-form varieties for Saturday. They always want to read, even when no one wants to hear them."

I laughed. "We'll call it a soft grand opening then. Maybe book some musicians for the following Saturday? How are the acoustics in here?"

"Amazing," Darren said softly. He must have seen the question in my look, because he continued sheepishly, "Guitar. I play in here sometimes after I've closed up the coffee shop."

No wonder Willow was infatuated with him.

~oOo~

I left Wicked Bean both elated and embarrassed. Thrilled to have a real job—the first one in a very long time that actually had meaning and would be helpful to others. But I'd clearly overwhelmed Darren, and it was beginning to dawn on me that Portlanders moved at a different pace than the D.C establishment. The people weren't in any way less intelligent; they just seemed to have different priorities. I could definitely get down with that—if I could just relax.

Per Roxy's suggestion, and with the help of my map, I found City Hall. I also found, however, that just being in the building raised my hackles back to my typical high-alert status. Politics, even in the procedural and administrative senses, is never a source of serenity.

But I forced myself to slip past the lethargic and obese armed security guard who was poorly disguised as an information desk attendant, climb the marble staircases, pop into offices, shake hands, smile, and spread my fresh business cards (printed in the wee hours of the morning) around. In a stroke of genius—I hoped—I'd added publicist to the list of services I was offering. I might also come to regret it, but the fabulous thing about being self-employed is that you can turn down work without having a boss yell at you for doing so.

There seemed to be a mid-morning lull in officialness, and people were genuinely friendly. Jovial laughter wafted down the halls, and several young staff members—interns probably—rushed around carrying indented cardboard trays loaded with steaming cups from the coffee shop on the first floor. It felt more like a Friday than the type of Monday I was accustomed to.

As I exited one of the offices, I collided with a broad belly. The man and I both said "Ooof."

"Whoa there, little..." his eyes, pale behind a pair of rimless eyeglasses, roamed upward, and he stopped himself from calling me a *little lady*. I knew it was on the tip of his tongue. He recovered quickly and stuck out his right hand, accompanied by a lecherous wink. "Commissioner Ross Perkins. It appears that I need to lose a little weight so both you and I can shimmy through the doorway at the same time."

There were so many things wrong with that statement, I couldn't even begin to count them. On the other hand, would it be reasonable to expect anything less insinuatingly offensive from a politician? But I didn't have time to indulge this particular peeve because I was terribly distracted by the man standing just behind the honorable Ross Perkins. Rude Ross kept babbling, but I tuned out the rest of his suggestive comments.

It was the measuring-wheel-and-clipboard man from the beach at the wildlife refuge. My heart was hammering in my chest, but the man didn't exhibit any signs that he recognized me. He did, however, also have his right hand extended. His lips moved, and I realized he was telling me his name too, trying to cut through the clutter of Ross's verbosity.

"Pardon?" Now I had two hands to shake. I awkwardly shifted my tote bag and went through the proper motions.

"Frank Cox," the man from the refuge repeated, "of Cox and Associates."

Ross laughed loudly. "This fellow owns half of the west side, got big developments out in Hillsboro, another one coming up off Cornelius Pass."

Mr. Cox had the decency to look humbly embarrassed. He probably practiced in front of a mirror. "It's not quite as bad as all that," he said with a smile, still holding my hand. "And you are?"

"Looking for work." I handed both men business cards, the quicker to make my getaway. I figured neither one would be willing to hire someone who sounded so desperate. Direct route to the circular file.

I hustled down the hall and punched the button for the elevator.

By the time I was safely sheltered in my old Volvo, I was feeling less flustered and regretted my burst of cynicism. I was beginning to wonder if I'd escaped D.C. too late, if I was irrevocably damaged by all the years I'd spent inside that grinding sphere of influence peddling. I'd been a bystander only, but the associated grime seemed to have penetrated too deeply to slough off in just a couple weeks. My entire outlook on life was skewed.

The answer, temporarily, was solitude in the car. Map on my lap, I explored the city. I found the airport and drove over several of the scenic bridges that cross the Willamette River. I also spent a lot of money at a couple home improvement stores. I had to hope that my business cards turned up at least a few additional jobs.

CHAPTER 7

Sloane called for the update I'd promised her as I was standing in the marina parking lot behind the open trunk of the Volvo with my hands on my hips, surveying the armloads of stuff I needed to trek across floating walkways to my house.

"Why'd I move here?" I whined into the phone.

"To be close to me, goofball," Sloane replied cheerfully.

"I know that." I grinned. "I mean here, as in floating house. I need Sherpas on permanent retainer."

"Can't help you there," Sloane said, "but I have a munchkin who's dying to tell you about her day at school."

And I just about died from the cuteness of it all. Little Ginger, at six years old, still thought school was fun, mostly. I held the phone to my ear and walked down the gangplank to get one of the marina's carts while Ginger chattered about crayons, recess, the alphabet song, and that stinky Joel Blum who wouldn't leave her alone. Apparently, Mrs. Willcott, the teacher, had made them both sit in a time-out while everyone else got to tear newspapers into strips for some kind of craft project. It had been the ultimate form of torture for Ginger, and she was still sore about it. Her rambling tales certainly put my stressful day into perspective.

Sloane was laughing when she returned to the phone. "Best therapy in the world, huh?"

"Thank you," I sighed. "I needed that."

"Let me know when the renovation projects get serious. I'll be over in my grubbies."

"You're on."

After I hung up, I realized I'd completely forgotten to tell Sloane about the dead man. But she was probably about to start preparing supper for her family. I decided the gruesome information could wait.

The third time I passed the scratched and dinged kayak that was lying on the edge of the walkway at slip A-3, I decided I wanted to buy it. A crude, hand-lettered sign on cardboard that said "FOR SALE $50" was propped on the seat. The kayak was a muddy, olive-drab color and had clearly seen better days. But it looked like it would accommodate my long legs.

The boat in slip A-3 had seen better days too. I don't know much about boats, but I could tell that this one was a sailboat, even though she was missing her mast. Her name, in faded paint on the stern, was *Ecclesiastes*. She was big—to me anyway, maybe thirty feet—and made of wood and had been a thing of beauty in her youth. But now I was rather surprised she was still capable of floating. I'd assumed she was someone's hobby project—a project that had been long neglected.

Where was the owner? The kayak hadn't been on the walkway when I'd left this morning, so I hoped he was around somewhere. I didn't dare go aboard the sailboat without permission. I wouldn't have wanted to take that risk, anyway.

I knelt on the walkway and stretched out to knock on the hull of the sailboat. It sounded empty and hollow and dull—and ineffectual. I knocked again, harder.

The door of the cabin swung open silently. A man—dirty, tanned, weathered, shaggy-haired, and scruffy—half emerged from the opening. His eyes were that bright blue that glitters in reflected sunlight. They were like marbles in his head. He didn't say anything, just stared.

"Uh, I'm interested in the kayak," I stammered.

He gave a slight nod. "Fifty bucks."

I'd been thinking about how much I'd already spent that day. And about the fact that I had only one real gig lined up. And exactly zero income at the moment. I sat back on my knees, safely away from the water I'd been leaning over. "Forty?" I squeaked.

And then I felt terrible. This man appeared to need the money worse than I did.

His eyes narrowed. "I heard you cook."

My mouth hung open. *Willow. Of course.* I nodded.

"You make brownies?" he asked.

I nodded again.

"Forty bucks," he agreed. "And I'll throw in the paddle and a life jacket if you bring me a big—and I mean *big*—pan of brownies in the next couple days."

I grinned at him. I'd been too dumb to even think that a paddle might not be included with the kayak. "Deal."

The sailboat swayed as he climbed the rest of the way out of the cabin and stepped off the edge of the boat onto the walkway. He was barefoot. "Eva." He said my name simply and familiarly and stuck out his right hand. "Cal Barclay."

I would never need to worry about introducing myself with Willow running around ahead of me.

I shook Cal's hand. Up close, he looked much younger and more physically fit. Early fifties, maybe, even though I couldn't see any gray in his light brown hair. Lean but also wiry strong. Still dirty, though, and very much in need of a haircut.

"Do you live aboard? I didn't see you at Bettina's party."

"Not usually invited to those shindigs," Cal said. No resentment, just a statement. His front teeth overlapped a little. Not badly enough to need braces. Kind of cute, actually.

He stepped back onto his boat, rummaged in a locker, and pulled out a life jacket and paddle. "I'll help haul the kayak down to your place."

And a gentleman, to boot. "Okay." I smiled at him. For all the grime, he didn't smell bad.

We settled the kayak on the rear deck. I'd be able to launch into the river straight off the deck. I was back to thinking that living in a floating house was a fabulous idea, even if it did require lots of hiking and packing.

I handed him two twenties from my wallet, and he stuffed the bills in his pocket with another slight nod. A man of few words.

Except he must have spotted the pressure washer I'd unloaded into a tangled heap on the deck and said, "Need help?"

Considering the condition of his boat, I wasn't sure I should admit that home repair was a little beyond my own skill set as well. So I shrugged. "Maybe."

"I like cheesecake too. And moussaka. Pork escalope. Not picky."

I tipped my head to study him more closely, but he turned on his heel and padded softly along the walkway. Was he was offering to work for food—in addition to the brownies? Was he that poverty-stricken? He wanted good food, though, not just basic sustenance. Not picky, huh? I felt a grin spreading across my face.

I'd left the marina cart at his slip, full of my stuff, so I had to follow him back. Cal had disappeared into his boat by the time I got there, and I carried on with carrying on—lug, lug, lug, tromp, tromp, tromp, back and forth.

Except on my fifth—and final—return trip, Vaughn was standing at the edge of slip A-3. There's no sneaking up on people at the marina. Footsteps reverberate on the walkways. The large number of empty slips and the low profiles of many of the boats that are stored year-round also provide lots of viewing gaps. First you hear people coming, then you see them, in short order.

Vaughn and Cal stood shoulder to shoulder, surveying the horizon like two casual statues, but their lips were moving. Vaughn spoke, Cal answered—back and forth in short, few-worded bursts. It appeared to be a comfortable conversation.

Both sets of eyes locked on me as I approached, so I gave them a sunny smile.

"Feeling better today, Ms. Fairchild?" Vaughn asked.

"Please call me Eva. Everyone else does."

Cal smirked a little behind the tan.

When I passed by, they fell in behind me. Two men abreast striding behind the girl with the cart.

The marina carts are a cross between wheelbarrows and wagons. They feel a little ridiculous, especially since I have to semi-stoop to reach the handle which means the front end of the cart rides up on my heels if I'm not careful when I'm pulling it. The whole procedure is ungainly and probably presents a rather unattractive rear view.

I channeled my inner supermodel (not!) and sallied forth, the cart bouncing and thumping across each wood plank. I sounded like an advancing army. But when I stowed the cart in the specially designated area at the base of the gangplank, Vaughn and Cal clanged up the gangplank without slowing.

They were up to something. Obviously. I doubted there was ever a time when Vaughn *wasn't* up to something, given his job. From what little I'd seen of Cal, on the other hand, I suspected he was most often *not* up to something. But together? Naturally, I was curious.

I'd left my map in the car—which is generally where maps belong. But it was an excellent excuse. I trotted up the gangplank after them.

When my head came level with the parking lot surface, I spotted them standing at the back of a white pickup truck with its tailgate down. The nose of a bright-orange kayak poked out of the end of the pickup's bed.

Fortunately, the pickup was parked right next to my Volvo.

"Yeah, that's it," Cal said as I stuck my key in the door lock.

My Volvo is ancient and has the rusty hinges to prove it. The driver's door screeches like a tomcat on the prowl every time I open it. I pretended not to notice and ducked my head inside.

"You sure?" Vaughn asked.

I tried to make removing the map from the door pocket last as long as possible, but it's a one-second job, no matter how you parse it. I stood back up and slammed the door closed, fast and hard, because the hinge screech the other direction is even worse than a tomcat—think a hyena in heat. I prefer to keep the agony as short as possible.

"Yep," said Cal, the man of few words.

Vaughn passed me on the way to the cab of the pickup. He climbed in and flashed the little, tilted, amused smile that kind of makes me crazy through the window. The engine roared to life, and he drove the truck through a wide arc toward the parking lot exit, the gravel crunching under the tires.

The resulting dust cloud didn't seem to bother Cal, but I clamped a hand over my nose. "Are you shopping for another kayak?" I asked.

"Already have one. But the one Vaughn has isn't for sale. It's evidence."

I turned and stared at his profile.

Cal answered as though I had voiced the question in my head. "Ian Thorpe"—he shifted, and his marble eyes bore into mine—"just turned into a murder investigation."

I gasped. "Did Vaughn tell you?"

"Didn't have to. Why else would he ask me to identify the man's kayak?"

~oOo~

It didn't quite add up to me. If Ian Thorpe had drowned, wouldn't the police still want to identify his kayak once it was found, just to verify that it didn't belong to some other unfortunate missing person they ought to be looking for?

But Cal knew things. For one, he knew how to identify a kayak. They all pretty much looked the same to me, but in different colors. Half the kayaks I'd seen out on the river the day before had been bright orange. If Cal knew Ian Thorpe's kayak, then it was pretty safe to assume he had also known Ian Thorpe himself.

I'd gotten the impression Cal had only relayed his conclusion because I had a vested interest, as though I was owed the information because I'd found the body. But there was also a tacit message, an undercurrent, that the information was not to be shared. That it was Vaughn's and he would be the one to have the say about when it was revealed publicly.

Which I totally understood. My lips were sealed, even though Cal hadn't explicitly asked for my confidentiality. I'd already witnessed the rapid transit of information within the marina—and outside of it, thanks to Willow. She couldn't be the only one, either. Everyone is fully capable of saying all kinds of things.

Regardless, Cal was getting his brownies as soon as humanly possible. I whacked a Lindt chocolate bar into pieces and stirred the extra-delicious bits into the eggs-oil-sugar-cocoa-flour mixture. Then I scooped the batter into a greased pan and popped it in the oven.

I settled on a barstool to lick the bowl and tackle Darren's promotional campaign. The kitchen peninsula was proving excellent for multitasking. By the time the brownies were perfectly crispy on the edges and gooey in the center, I had the first set of mock-ups prepared to send to Darren.

When the brownie pan was cool enough to carry, I covered it with foil and made the delivery. Once again, I had to kneel, stretch off the edge of the boardwalk, and knock on the hull of his sailboat.

Cal had the look of a man who'd found the fountain of youth when he peeled back the foil and inhaled. "Damn," he muttered. "I think I'll be able to stand having you for a neighbor."

I decided to put that comment to the test. "What's tomorrow look like for you?"

"Wide open."

"Because that pressure washer isn't going to run itself. Could you show me how to use it?" The salesclerk at the equipment rental place had spent about two minutes pointing at various parts, and he'd spoken words that I'd recognized as English only about half of that time. I'd been planning on looking up the instructions online, but an in-person tutorial would be even better.

"Yep."

~oOo~

It turned out that pressure washing is kind of fun, even addicting in a weird sort of way. It probably helped that the exterior of my house was so dirty and flaky that a few blasts with the nozzle made immediate and impressive improvements.

But my arms got tired. Wobbly, jiggly, like wet noodles. Cal offered to pick up where I left off, and he seemed to enjoy the process too. We settled on a full pan of lasagna as suitable remuneration—to be presented sometime in the next few days. I loved his negotiation style. If I worked it out right, I might be able to have Willow practice her cooking on Cal while I served as the instructor and quality control inspector.

With Cal blasting the outside of my house with water, I was able to work inside, finishing up a series of samples for Darren based on his feedback. I sent them as attachments to an email and then texted him to make sure he'd have a moment to check them over. Then I left a message with the event reporter at Portland's alternative weekly newspaper, *Willamette Week*, about the soft grand opening of the Wicked Bean Annex on Saturday. Why pay for advertising when you can get a free write-up that also helps the reporter fill her allotted space?

Willow came skipping down the walkway after school, just as Cal was reeling up the pressure washer hose. He was soaked to the skin, T-shirt and cargo shorts clinging to his lean body, but he didn't seem to mind. I didn't see a single goose bump on him.

But he reminded me of a dog that's had a bath, when its hairy fluff is exposed for just that and you can see the scrawny frame underneath. I'd known Cal was slender and wiry, but now his physique was particularly evident. Corded veins stood out in his forearms, and his calves were knots of muscle. The man's body fat percentage was in the low, very low, single digits.

"Hey, you bought Cal's kayak," Willow announced. The girl misses not one iota. Since the kayak was still on the rear deck, out of her immediate view, it's also possible that she has X-ray vision.

"Want to go for a trial run—or trial paddle?" I asked her. "I need a backup in case I tip over."

"You won't." Cal finished returning the pressure washer to a neater state than it had been in when I'd rented it. "That style of kayak is the most stable there is."

"Or get lost," I amended.

His blue eyes glinted. "Well, there is that."

"Thank you," I called after him.

He waved without turning as he padded, barefoot, along the walkway toward his slip.

"You really want to?" Willow asked.

"Yes. Unless you have homework—or something."

Willow snorted, the answer I'd been hoping to hear. "I'll be right back." Then she tore down the walkway at nowhere near the sedate pace Cal had employed.

She returned ten minutes later via water. She held my kayak pressed against the edge of the deck with her paddle while I cautiously lowered myself into it. "Let's head upriver first in case you poop out. That way it'll be easier coming back."

I grinned at her. "A fount of wisdom."

Willow snorted. "Just the voice of experience which belies my age."

Which was true, unfortunately. I hated that she'd been put in a position where she had to grow up extra fast. But there was still a lot of young insecurity under that blue-haired exterior. I informed her that her next cooking lesson would be lasagna.

"For Cal?" We were paddling side by side, and I was certain she was holding back her pace so I could keep up. Her face turned scrunchy for a moment—not from exertion—and then she asked. "Do you think he's starving?"

"Not if we can help it."

"He's weird, you know."

"Aren't we all?"

Willow snorted again. "Word, sister."

I wasn't entirely up on hip-hop lingo, but I knew what she meant. "Cal, though—what's the scoop?" Since she'd told other people about me, then surely she could tell me about other people.

The gentle swell of the water was relaxing, and while we weren't going anywhere fast, the paddling was pretty easy too. The first lights along the banks were winking on in the dusk. Bird calls, a low motor noise in the distance. It felt like we were on the planet, but not of it— removed to a peaceful observation post accompanied by the rhythmic, soft splashes of dipping paddles. It was like being in a bubble or cocoon, and I was seriously enamored of kayaking already.

"CIA," Willow said, catching me off guard.

I'd been so distracted that I hadn't realized she was taking an unusually long time to answer. "What?" I blurted.

"Former CIA, I guess. That's the rumor, anyway. He never talks about himself, but he knows lots of stuff. Survival stuff, world politics stuff, travel stuff, bugs you can eat, how to do bizarre stuff that isn't in anybody's normal range of activities, you know?"

I reminded myself that this assessment came from a girl who hadn't known until two days ago that onions had to be peeled before they could be eaten.

"Doc says Cal must have been in Southeast Asia for a long time. Probably got sick there. Maybe parasites. Maybe that's why he's like permanently tanned and so gaunt. He knows lots about boats and navigation, and he goes barefoot almost all the time, even in winter."

"He doesn't get invited to social events?" I asked.

"Bettina tried at first, but he always said no. He just stays in his boat and barely talks to anyone. I think he mostly goes out at night." Willow shrugged. "He's nice enough, I guess. Not creepy, but he's basically a hermit."

I wanted to ask her why or how Vaughn knew that Cal would be able to identify Ian Thorpe's kayak, but that reminded me that we were doing exactly the same thing Ian had been when he'd been killed—allegedly. Or not so allegedly since I really didn't know. But there was no point in causing Willow to associate kayaking with death by bringing it up.

I didn't want to think about it myself. The river was entirely too peaceful for such macabre musings. I picked up my pace a notch. "Race you."

Which was a mistake. Willow whipped ahead, and I was soon panting in her wake.

She stopped and let me catch up with her just off what appeared to be a new development on the east riverbank.

"What is this?" I wheezed, and waved to indicate the huge concrete pumping booms that loomed over rebar cages and the hulking shapes of heavy equipment—dump trucks, backhoes, and other things I couldn't identify in the gloom or didn't know the names of.

"Some kind of upscale, exclusive property. Condos, restaurants, some retail shops, I guess. They're making a mess of the riverbank, had to get special permits to build a retaining wall to prevent erosion from undermining the buildings they're going to put at the edge of the water." Willow rested her paddle across her lap and drifted beside me. "Big brouhaha. A bunch of community meetings with people yelling at each other. Gran went to one. The company that owns the land has lots of money in it, so they want to get their investment back. But there are going to be a bunch of displaced river otters too. Not to mention increased traffic. Everybody has an opinion about it, so I try not to mention it." I couldn't tell for sure in the growing darkness, but I think she rolled her eyes in disgust at the inability of adults to get along with one other. Age doesn't improve some things.

"I haven't seen a river otter yet. Are they cute?"

"Yeah. They're kind of a nuisance too. They tear apart the Styrofoam blocks that make the marina walkways float to line their dens. Gran's always grumbling about it because those blocks are so expensive to replace. We even had a Fish & Wildlife guy come out to try to trap the otters that were destroying our blocks so they could be relocated. They have a sixth sense about it, though. No otters ever went in the traps even though he baited them with cat food and salmon and gummy bears. He only caught a few raccoons and one bedraggled cat that just about clawed his arm off when he let it out."

"Gummy bears?" I laughed.

"What can I say?" Willow chuckled too. "Otters like sweets. At least, they're supposed to. But not inside cages apparently."

We'd let the current carry us back downriver, past a couple parallel rows of broken pilings, relics from an abandoned set of docks, and now we were bobbing offshore from the wildlife refuge—a long, dark patch of tall trees and wet sand. It looked both forlorn and foreboding, a wild scraggle of woods surrounded by creeping urban sprawl. I wondered if the animals sheltered there for the night felt the encroachment on their territory.

My phone rang, splitting the darkness with an incredibly obnoxious noise and flash of LED screen that was visible through the fabric of my sweatshirt pocket.

Willow groaned and flicked water at me with her paddle. "Way to ruin the setting."

"Sorry," I whispered, then I raised my voice slightly to answer the phone, "Hello?"

"Ms. Fairchild?" said a very pleasant, feminine voice. "I'm Lila Halton. I work for a real estate consulting and management firm, and I picked up one of your business cards at City Hall. I'm sorry to call so late, but we have a rather urgent matter to deal with, and we need more hands on deck. We need someone with your expertise."

CHAPTER 8

Expertise? I started to laugh out loud, but managed to partially choke it back. Instead, my amusement came out like a gurgle.

"Of course," I replied after I'd taken a deep breath. But it was difficult to sound professional when Willow was smacking the flat side of her paddle on the water like a fretful beaver. I tried to shove her kayak with my own paddle but couldn't reach. "Can I call you back in about fifteen minutes? I'll have my laptop then and will be prepared to take notes."

That's when I learned to paddle quickly. Willow gave me a few terse pointers and stayed abreast of me as I flailed away.

"You really need the job, huh?" she asked.

"Isn't it obvious?"

Once again, she held my kayak in position as I wriggled my fanny out of the seat and up onto the deck. "Thanks," I muttered.

She grunted, her face pale in the light cast by the lampposts on the walkway. I couldn't tell if her sour expression was caused by my cutting our outing short or just general teenage moodiness. She swung the end of her kayak wide and paddled away without a word.

I secured my kayak on the deck and darted inside. I grabbed a handful of necessary supplies and plugged in my laptop. For a moment, I squeezed my eyes closed and steadied my breathing so I could present the facade of calm, cool, and collected. Then I dialed Lila's number.

I needn't have worried because what she required most urgently was a sympathetic ear, and I spent the next half hour listening. She did, indeed, have an extraordinary situation on her hands. There were a few things I couldn't bring myself to interrupt her to say—like the fact that I was aware of a few more of the pertinent details than she was. In this particular matter, I actually did have some inside knowledge, if not expertise. Not that I'd wanted them, but the impressions in my memory were irrevocable now.

Lila wasn't panicking—yet—but she needed to hear that her responses were normal, that she wasn't crazy, that her problem could be handled. I made reassuring noises and murmured soothingly. In the end, I understood why she wanted to hire an outsider without previous connection to her client—Cox and Associates—and I agreed to develop a communications strategy and write press releases as they became necessary. Because I was relying on the assumption that a company couldn't or wouldn't kill a man.

According to the nightly news, people commit murder, usually individually or as part of a small scheme, but generally, collective entities don't. Unless you're talking about a manufacturing or mining pollution disaster with long-term catastrophic health effects on the local population. But that wasn't the case here. Here, we were talking about Ian Thorpe.

I was sitting on a barstool, staring off into space and pondering my new life as a publicist when a quiet tapping sounded on the door.

Detective Vaughn Malloy appeared exceedingly long and oddly bulbous in the peephole.

Just the man I'd wanted to see. Because if I wasn't extremely careful with this mess, I'd be following in my father's footsteps, and I was absolutely determined not to do that. I let him in.

"Studying the scene again?" I asked.

He shrugged. "Had a few more questions for Cal. Saw your light was on."

Have I mentioned that he smells good? Spicy, like cloves—or really good carnations that haven't been stripped of all their personality by over-breeding. But he certainly wasn't a flowery sort of man. Maybe a little peppermint or eucalyptus in there somewhere. I resisted the urge to lean closer and sniff.

Instead, I studied the long lines of his face. "You need more than coffee. When was the last time you ate?"

Another shrug. "I seem to recall a bagel mid-morning."

I clucked and tugged him toward the kitchen. "Sit." I pointed to the barstool I'd just vacated and tidied my notepapers and laptop into a pile. "I haven't eaten yet either. So I'm not doing you a favor; I'd be cooking anyway. Twenty minutes."

I started by making coffee, just to tide him over, before I strapped an apron around my waist. Then I cubed new potatoes, sliced bacon, chopped green onion, and melted my favorite ingredient of all time—butter. When I gaged that the scent rising from the frying pan was too irresistible for him to flee, I launched into the monologue I'd been diagramming in my head.

"I just got a job. Publicity, spin, damage control—whatever you want to call it. Three degrees of separation." I ticked the sequence of relationship off on my fingers. "Ian Thorpe, environmental activist and sworn antagonist of Cox and Associates because of that mixed-use complex they're building just south of the wildlife refuge; Cox and Associates, the real estate development company that hypothetically has an excellent reputation in the area, according to their lobbyist, because of their concern for the environment, the principal of which—Frank Cox—is a significant taxpayer, both personally and through his company, and a well-known consort to city council members and county commissioners; Lila Halton, lobbyist who looks after the political and business interests of Cox and Associates; me, newbie hired by Lila Halton to do the same but in the sphere of public opinion."

I took a deep breath. It had all made sense in my head, but now I felt like I needed some graph paper to chart out the relationships with little directional arrows. Some of the arrows would crisscross, because the whole thing was rather circular, mainly for the one reason both Vaughn and I knew about but I hadn't yet mentioned in this particular context. So I added, "Also me, finder of Ian Thorpe's body."

"Cal would have found him if you hadn't. Just a matter of timing," Vaughn said rationally. He stretched across the counter and spun the French press handle toward himself. He refilled his mug and slurped from it, apparently not feeling the need to say anything further.

So I was left with stating the obvious. "Which means I now officially have a reason—beyond the personal one—for being exceedingly nosy about the case. You're probably going to need to stay away from me."

"You think I can't resist your charms—professionally, of course?" His smile was more than a tilt this time. I could actually see the hint of an even set of teeth behind the lips. Orthodontia at some point in his past—I'd be willing to bet on it.

I scowled at him, barely resisting the type of snort Willow usually emits. That girl was rubbing off on me. "On the contrary. I just wanted to be completely up-front with you about my motives and goals." I turned to the stove and gave the contents of the frying pan a stern jostle. This conversation was not going how I'd planned. My public relations skills definitely needed some work.

Maybe if he knew...so I kept talking while cracking eggs into the hash. "My father's a lobbyist too. He represents various big industry interests in D.C. Which means cronyism galore. I hate what he does, because he's not so honest. Not exactly dishonest, technically, but there's a lot of strategic omission in his line of work. I told myself I'd never be like him." I sprinkled fresh spinach leaves over the conglomeration in the pan and slammed a lid on it.

I turned to find Vaughn's warm brown eyes following my every move. "Which is why I'm telling you," I finished.

Vaughn nodded slightly. "Fair enough." He gestured with his coffee mug before finishing off the last gulp. "Technically, this could be considered bribery, then. Sounds like I'm walking a fine ethical edge just sitting on this stool drinking your coffee."

And then I did snort. I couldn't help it. "Better get out while you can." I slid the hash onto two plates and waved one under his nose. "Because this is about to get really good."

He captured the plate, his hands wrapping over mine, and he carefully released it from my grip. "I'll take my chances. My chief's pretty lenient when it comes to nutrition." The corners of his eyes crinkled up. And then his stomach growled—so loudly that we both laughed.

I came around the bar and slid onto the stool next to him. We ate in silence for several minutes.

Finally, I worked up the nerve to ask the question that had been blaring in my mind—the one I'd have to address in my first press release. "Did you know that Ian Thorpe hated Cox and Associates?"

"I do now, and not because you told me." Vaughn cast a sidelong glance at me before spearing several potatoes on his fork. "I searched his apartment today. Standard procedure in an investigation of this nature. So I've skimmed through his possessions and paperwork."

"Speaking of that—murder—" I took a moment to swallow so I wouldn't gross him out. "How long have you known? And does the public know? I'm going to have to wait until you announce it, so when do you expect that to be? Lila didn't know, and it was hard not telling her. It makes her client—my client—look even worse."

Vaughn's brown eyes widened, just slightly, but enough. I'd been a dork to even ask. But I wouldn't be doing my job if I didn't.

He wiped his mouth with a napkin and regarded me thoughtfully. "Cal must have told you." His eyes narrowed and he turned back to his plate. "No matter. That was why I stopped by tonight. You have a right—personally—to know. Tomorrow morning, nine o'clock. The announcement will come from the medical examiner at a police press conference. Short and to the point, no comment. And never, ever any speculation."

"Of course," I murmured. But I mentally adjusted my schedule for the following day.

A loud rapping on the front door made me jump. Vaughn's head popped up, and we stared at each other for a moment. I thought about making a snarky comment about my popularity, especially at supper time, but tamped it down and shuffled to the door.

Bettina Godinou. I could barely see her in the peephole—she was so short—but the orange hair was unmistakable.

"Your mother," I hissed.

Vaughn looked stricken, panicky almost, but just for a second. "She can't see me here," he whispered back. He stood by the stool uncertainly, hand on the counter.

"Take your plate—quick. In the bedroom." I pointed toward the dark doorway off the short hall.

He blinked. "I can't go in your bedroom. Not—"

"I don't sleep in there, remember? Don't be so squeamish." I flapped my hands at him as if that would make him move faster. While floating houses might have back doors, the escape routes don't exactly lead anywhere—unless one wants to swim.

He bolted into action, scooping up his plate and silverware and balancing his mug on top of the pile. He was a rapidly disappearing shadow when I flung open the front door.

I blocked the opening with my body and stared down at the intruder. "Bettina."

"Did the bangles work? I want to know if you got the job."

I exhaled. Was that all? It took tremendous mental effort to change the direction of my thoughts. "Marvelously. In fact, I now have two jobs."

Bettina clasped her hands together and bounced on her toes. In her richly-embroidered tunic and skinny leggings, she looked alarmingly like the freakish clown that pops out of a jack-in-the-box. "I knew it," she exclaimed. "I brought you more." She wriggled past me and headed straight for the kitchen bar peninsula, a cloth bag dangling from her bent elbow. So much for my attempt at guard duty. I hoped Vaughn was chewing the remainder of his hash very quietly in the bedroom.

"You're eating?" Bettina wrinkled her nose.

"Like most people I know," I replied.

She shoved my plate out of the way and proceeded to arrange her offerings on the counter. They consisted of a choker collar in intricate metal scrollwork, three chunky rings, four pairs of gigantic dangly earrings, and another smattering of bracelets.

"Bettina, really," I protested. "I rarely wear jewelry. I find it too constraining."

"Nonsense. Besides, I have too much inventory. It has to go somewhere."

You could stop making it, I wanted to say, but held my tongue. Maybe it was the only hobby she had.

"These earrings will look good with that yellow sundress you were wearing the other day. You like warm colors, right? Bronze, copper, natural materials? I have some beautiful polished wood beads that I could work up into a long, twisty necklace for you. Maybe some coral..." She tapped her chin while examining the glittering array on the counter.

"You're overwhelming me. Really," I insisted. "My self-protection instincts, which involve running—and sometimes screaming—in the opposite direction, are threatening to kick in."

I meant it as a joke, but Bettina flinched as if startled and peered up at me. "You do that too?" she squeaked. "Because that's what I'm doing. My coping mechanism is to dump perfectly useless jewelry on people and scrub my bathtub."

I laughed and stuck out my hand. "Truce?"

She sighed and shook hands with me. Then she swept all the jewelry back into the cloth pouch. "But you're keeping the bangles," she said.

"Yes. Thank you." I tried to make my tone sound more grateful than I was feeling at the moment. "So why are you really here?"

"To apologize for my snively distress the other night. You just moved in, and I realize I was laying it on pretty thick for a brand new acquaintance."

I patted her arm. "It's all right. It was a big decision."

"Which I should have made much sooner, as you so wisely pointed out. Nigel is history."

"I'm glad to hear it." I set the frying pan in the sink and squirted dish soap into it. I clattered the rest of my utensils together and dropped them into the sink too, trying to make as much noise as possible. I was very aware that an extra pair of ears was sitting in my bedroom, and I had a feeling Bettina was about to divulge information she'd rather her son not know.

"Norman's coming for dinner on Friday night. What should I make for him?"

Suddenly, lifting the grates on the stove top and wiping off all the butter splatters seemed important. "Your Facebook friend? A knuckle sandwich." Clang, bang, thump, swoosh.

Bettina tittered and wiped at the corner of her eye with a manicured finger. "You're hilarious. No, seriously. I want to impress him."

I opened the fridge and stuck my head inside under the pretext of returning ingredients to their rightful storage spots, hoping all that extra insulation would muffle my words. "Steak and potatoes. Nothing green if you can help it. Cheesecake." Maybe Norman would keel over from a heart attack and spare Bettina the agony of another mangled relationship. Of course, my suggestion was awfully similar to what I'd just served Vaughn—and eaten myself—with the exception of the spinach.

"You don't think that's too much of a come-on?" Bettina asked.

I hit my head on a refrigerator shelf and backed out of the cold compartment. "Surely you're still in the getting-to-know-each-other stage?" My voice cracked. "He'll only think it's a come-on if you make some kind of physical move, won't he?" But what did I know?

Bettina's face was puckered awkwardly, and I realized her expression mirrored my own uncertainty. We were a pair of romantically clueless women.

I shook my head. "Actually, I can't help you there. Why don't you cancel? You could develop flu symptoms."

"But I like this one." Bettina was starting to sound miffed. "He's going to review my investment portfolio and see if I'm in the right risk category for my age."

"Sounds like a dreamboat," I muttered.

"I think you're jealous," Bettina announced. "You really should find yourself a man." She flounced off the stool and headed for the front door.

My mouth hung open, but I managed to follow her, like an automaton hostess seeing her guest off.

"Ta-ta," Bettina called. "You should think it over, dear. Just let me know. I can arrange dinner with my son, Vaughn, whenever you like."

I exhaled and quietly clicked the door closed. At least she hadn't suspected that Vaughn was actually under my roof at that very moment. Whew.

"What was that all about?" The baritone voice sounded awfully close. One of the joys of a small house. Which, I might point out, only matters when there's more than one person in the aforementioned house. I rather liked the coziness of my accommodations—when I was alone.

I spun around. "Uh, I can't tell you?" What I'd intended as an emphatic statement came out sounding as though I was asking his permission. I frowned and added more severely, "How much did you hear?"

"Every word. You can't tell me, huh?" That infuriatingly endearing tilted smile was playing at the edge of his lips again as he slid his dishes into the sudsy water.

I shook my head. "Sworn to secrecy. Perhaps we should talk about why you're more afraid of your own mother than of your boss, the chief of police, and his ethical guidelines."

Vaughn chuckled. "Not open for discussion. But you seem pretty good at guessing. Would *you* have wanted her to find us together—eating together? You think she's meddlesome now..." He didn't have to finish the sentence. His wry grin spoke volumes. "It wouldn't have mattered that our tête-a-tête tonight was part of an investigation."

I thought he was stretching the rationalizing a little too far. We'd barely discussed Ian Thorpe's murder, mainly because *he* couldn't discuss it, at least not with me. But I'd grant him that excuse if he wanted it—I'd probably have to cop the same plea myself if Bettina ever found out about my duplicity—and nodded in reluctant agreement. "You're lucky this time."

"I knew about Nigel, by the way. But now it's Norman, huh?" Vaughn said.

"Rather dashing, apparently. With a head for numbers." I planted my fists on my hips. "Can you run a background check on him?"

"Not *ethically*." Vaughn let the word roll off his tongue.

And with a sharp lurch in my stomach I realized how much I really—and I mean really, really—liked his mouth. So much that I was staring at it. Openly—and he'd caught me. Blast.

He edged past me on the way to the door. "If it makes your job any easier, Frank Cox has an alibi for the majority of the time span during which the medical examiner estimates Thorpe died," he said in a low voice.

"But—" I spluttered.

"Tomorrow at nine. Maybe I'll see you there?" And Vaughn was gone, solidly latching the door behind him.

CHAPTER 9

Ooooo. That man. How irritating. He had a wealth of details about the investigation—we both knew it. But dropping that particular detail and then skipping out? Dastardly.

Also relieving. At least now I could work, if indirectly, for Frank Cox without injuring my poor little conscience. But that didn't prevent my mind from devolving into a jumble of questions.

Vaughn hadn't thanked me for the meal. Maybe somehow not acknowledging it made up for the unethicalness of eating food prepared by an involved party? If it even was unethical. If we'd called it a date, would sharing a meal and each other's company have been permissible then?

Enough already. I forced myself to clean up the rest of the dishes and go through the motions of preparing for bed.

After I was in my pajamas, I flicked on the overhead light in the bedroom. Vaughn hadn't left any visible trace of his temporary occupation. I sniffed, just to make sure. Nope. There was no respectable reason why I should feel disappointed about the absence of his scent. I snapped off the light.

I trudged up the stairs and stood in the darkness against the glass wall, looking out over my corner of the marina. It really was pretty—with the lampposts lining the walkways and their light reflecting off the rippling water and the dappled boats gently swaying in their berths.

There was a warm, yellow glow shining through the cabin porthole of Cal's sailboat, and I recalled Vaughn's assurance that Cal would have found the body if I hadn't.

For all his reclusive tendencies, Cal seemed to be acutely aware of the marina's happenings, perhaps even more so on a nocturnal basis. On an impulse, I lifted my arm and waved.

The light in Cal's cabin blinked off and on three times.

~oOo~

The Fidelity police station was of modern and ultra-practical concrete-bunker construction dressed up with lick-and-stick stone veneer on the side that faced the street. Somebody had thought to plunk a few shrubs in the ground outside the main entrance, but the paltry greenery didn't do much to aesthetically offset the blank surrounding expanse of asphalt parking lot.

It was a good thing I arrived early, because I nabbed the third to last open seat in the back row of chairs in the conference room. It wasn't a large room, and a wide swath along the rear wall had been reserved for television crews. They had their equipment and extensions cords strung all over the place.

"Eva?" A petite young woman dressed in brown corduroy pants and a trim chambray button-down shirt slid into the seat next to me. Her blonde hair was pulled back in a tight bun which she'd secured with a number-two pencil. Hazel eyes regarded me through a pair of stylishly retro, teal-framed glasses. "Lila," she informed me, even though it wasn't necessary. I recognized her voice from our multiple phone calls.

"Thanks for coming." She leaned closer, whispering, "Frank wants talking points immediately after the press conference. Three news stations have already asked him for interviews. Normally he does really well at off-the-cuff comments, but it's important this time for him to sound...well, appropriate."

"Concerned? Saddened? Eager for justice but respectfully confident in the abilities of the investigators?" With a reassuring smile, I waggled a notepad where I'd already jotted a few of the classic lines. "I'm on it. Is there a fund—perhaps a trust set up for the next of kin—that he could donate to? I also think it'd be admirable for Frank to openly acknowledge the tension that sometimes existed between Ian and himself and to emphasize that he welcomed their ideological differences in an iron-sharpens-iron sort of way."

"That's good. I'll give Frank a heads-up and let him mull it over," Lila breathed. We needn't have worried about being overheard because the television crews were making enough racket to cover an air-raid siren, but she tilted even closer until our shoulders bumped, still whispering. "The next of kin thing is a problem though. There's an ex-wife with whom Ian had a son. There's also a slew of ex-girlfriends and two other women who are both claiming to be the current girlfriend."

My brows shot up. This information—obviously—hadn't been included on the websites I'd visited in an attempt to find out about the person who'd lived in the body I'd found. It wasn't the sort of glowing character reference a nonprofit organization would boast about. Ian Thorpe sounded a great deal like another man I knew. Unfortunately, my family background had provided ample experience in the tricky art of maneuvering through a sea of disgruntled women.

I nodded slowly. "Numerous suspects, then."

Lila smiled grimly and offered a who-knows? shrug in response. She ducked down the aisle and settled into a seat in the second row beside a sandy-haired man in business attire. Even from the back he oozed affluence. It was Frank Cox—on his best behavior, apparently. And it was my job to make sure he had the tools necessary to maintain that impression.

Soon the space became cramped, standing-room only. The air was muggy with the odors of stress perspiration, bitter coffee, and fast food breakfasts eaten too quickly. The reporters and camera operators murmured and prepped, clanking their equipment and swapping caustic jokes behind me.

A door opened at the side of the front of the room, and a line of official-looking people dressed to match their occupations strode in. A few of the men took seats at the long table that was studded with microphones. Even more crammed in behind the designated speakers.

Vaughn was there—closest to the door, arms stiff at his sides, with a blank gaze directed well over the heads of the assembled information vultures. He was clearly uncomfortable with the rigmarole and was keeping his escape route open. He probably had his toes dug into the industrial carpet for traction, prepared to bolt as soon as a reasonable excuse presented itself. He looked like a truculent, overgrown child who'd been dressed up in his Sunday best against his expressed wishes. But the suit hung well across his shoulders, and the deep brown herringbone set off his eyes and features quite handsomely.

I briefly considered dialing his cell phone number and making a false report about some emergency just to give him the opportunity to skip out of the pending torture. But a stint in jail for falsifying a police report wouldn't do me any good on the personal income-generating front.

The man seated at the center of the table—wearing the dress blues, badge, and bulky gun belt of a hands-on police chief—cleared his throat into the bank of microphones. We all jumped to attention, wincing at the blast.

Then he rambled for five minutes—the concise dissemination of information not being his forte, but I also thought the impression was perhaps intentional in this particular situation—while loosely referring to a sheet of paper which he held tipped in front of him. He didn't present any facts I didn't already know.

Next, the man in the lab coat—the medical examiner—spoke. And this is when the juicy bits started coming out, in dry professional detail—or what passed for detail when a body had been in the water for several days.

Time of death: sometime in the twenty-four hours following when Ian was last seen on Tuesday night, but most likely earlier in that time period rather than later.

Cause of death: drowning. But—and this was huge—Ian had been unconscious when he'd entered the water. Hence, murder, or at the very least, manslaughter.

I bit my lip and scribbled furiously. The police must have been able to rule out suicide and accident. How? But both the chief and ME had been tight-lipped, sparing only a few tidbits that hadn't already been public knowledge. Perhaps I could learn more from what wasn't said than from the bare outline of facts they'd been willing to divulge.

The third man at the table took his turn. He was the executive director of the Friends of River Otters, dressed appropriately in jeans and plaid flannel shirt and about two-years' worth of beard, behind which I couldn't even see his lips moving. He was grieving for his friend, and, with difficulty, he read a compiled statement from several of the environmental groups Ian had supported and/or been instrumental in organizing.

I was a little surprised this guy had a place at the table. But he also represented the human interest side of the equation, and perhaps it saved time, because when they opened up the floor for questions, the reporters directed most of their initial barrage at him.

Then the questioning turned into a scattershot melee. The medical examiner immediately became exasperated with the inane and redundant questions the reporters kept lobbing at him. Finally, he resorted to dully stating "I already answered that" or "I can't comment on that aspect" or "unknown at this time" over and over again. He took to staring at a spot where the wall met the ceiling in the back of the room, in much the same way Vaughn had been—and continued to be—occupied.

I shifted on the hard metal folding chair and recrossed my legs. TB had set in with a vengeance. My hand was still cramped even though I'd stopped taking notes a while ago. Impatient irritation prickled up the back of my neck, but it was too crowded for me to wriggle my way out of the row without causing a scene. Plus, I was getting paid to be present, numb bottom or not.

By this point, the only people who actually wanted to be in that room were the reporters, who seemed to be basking in the glow of their own verbosity. But when they turned their attention to the chief of police, he quickly cut them short.

He answered three questions that had already been asked a dozen times then stood abruptly. "No further questions. There will be another press conference if and when more information comes to light." He turned and marched out the side door.

My hero.

Who started a stampede. Suddenly everyone seemed desperate for fresh air, including the reporters.

As though it was the baton in a relay race, I extended an arm and stretched to slip a tidy sheet of prioritized talking points to Lila as she and Frank squeezed through the crush blocking the rear doorway. She flapped the paper in thanks and mouthed, "Talk later."

I decided to hang around for a few minutes just in case. Lila had looked a little peaked, and she was tiny. She was Frank's handler, for lack of a better term, so she didn't need me lurking at the edge of the camera-shot framing for his television interviews. She'd be taking care of that herself—functioning as a blend of bodyguard, human teleprompter, and moral supporter. But I wanted to make sure she was up to the task, physically, and be ready to step in for her if needed.

I palmed my phone so I was prepared for an emergency call from Lila, but turned the other way, deeper along the deserted halls of the police station. It was like the quiet after a storm. I could hear the central heating system whooshing and clicking, trying to recover from the mass of warm bodies that had suddenly exited.

It seems that I am very good at bumping into people in doorways. This time, though, it wasn't a broad belly but rather a tall and firm torso in brown herringbone accompanied by a steadying grip around my elbow.

"Eva. So you made it." If it was even possible, Vaughn smelled better than he had the previous night.

"Highlight of my day," I grumbled.

"Maybe I can change that. How about lunch?"

I scowled up at him. "Already? It's not even ten o'clock in the morning."

He shrugged. "I didn't get a lot to eat yesterday. Gotta make up for it somehow."

I had my mouth open for a smart reply about his eating me out of house and home when I saw that he was laughing at me. Quietly. In fact, just with his eyes. But before I could readjust to an escalated level of indignant sarcasm, he tugged on my hand. "Come meet the chief."

People have so many layers. For most, I have no desire to learn what's beneath the surface. But with the rare few, it's an indescribable pleasure, an experience to be treasured, when they let you see who they really are. Lonnie Monk, chief of the Fidelity Police Department, was just such a person. I instantly knew why Vaughn hadn't been worried about offending his chief's ethical sensibilities.

There was an easy camaraderie between the two men. Not the hearty, back-slapping type of kinship, but more of a personal courtesy and respect, a quiet confidence and familiarity with one another. It was the only time in my life that I'd sensed such a strong absence of tension between two people. Oh—except with Sloane and me. We had it too, but I'd never witnessed it between other people before.

The chief was old enough to be Vaughn's father—mid-sixties or thereabouts. And maybe their relationship held an element of the father-son bond; or mentor-mentee; or perhaps a type of apprenticeship where the pupil now matches his tutor for knowledge and experience, with the assurance of knowing the transfer has been completed satisfactorily and beneficially. I would have to noodle away at what I was observing for a while before I'd be able to categorize it.

"Your first body?" Chief Monk asked while he shook my hand. It seemed to be a popular question in law enforcement circles.

"Of the dead sort, yes," I answered.

"Not the first at Marten's Marina, though. The way the currents in the river work, that's where floaters often end up. Roxy and I have held vigil several times there over the years, waiting for the ME's technicians to arrive. How's Roxy doing, by the way?" Chief Monk crossed his arms over his middle and rocked back at the hips into the classic cop stance.

Considering I'd only known Roxy for a few days, I settled on, "Persevering."

Chief Monk chuckled. "Yep. She's been doing that for years too. Give her my best. You two better get out of here while you can. Who knows what kind of scrum that media-fest in the parking lot is going to turn into." He gave me a curt nod and exited through a heavy metal door that banged behind him, but not before I'd caught a glimpse of a police cruiser with its hood up, undergoing an oil change.

"The garage," Vaughn muttered. "It's his second office."

I arched my brows in a silent question.

Vaughn broke into a full grin. "Where he goes when he doesn't want to answer the phone. One of the perks of being chief—the mechanic can't kick him out."

We rode in Vaughn's pickup. There was still a cluster of reporters and camera operators around the media vans in one corner of the parking lot, but I didn't spot Lila's small blonde head or Frank's sandy-brown one among the crowd. The crews appeared to be packing up.

Vaughn eased his truck out onto the street and drove down Fidelity's short retail corridor and then into one of the ramshackle residential areas. The front yards we passed were characterized by plastic children's toys scattered behind chain-link fences and the occasional barking dog of desultory lineage. Beyond the dilapidated neighborhood, he pulled up in front of a derelict commercial building that housed a pawnshop, a beauty salon, and—in a tiny space at the end—a taquería.

That segment of the building was stuccoed and painted adobe-red for ambiance, with twenty empty picnic tables lined up in the weedy lot next door. Strings of faded Corona and Nigra Modelo beer pennants were looped on tall poles and crisscrossed over the tables as though the place doubled as a finish line for a marathon. All that was missing was a bunch of gasping, sweaty people in spandex. It did not look promising.

But I kept my mouth shut. Maybe Vaughn really liked my company. Or maybe he didn't want to eat alone and would tolerate just about any type of fraternization to ameliorate his digestive process. If this hole-in-the-wall eatery was my competition in the culinary arts category, then Vaughn was far less discriminating than I had expected.

He pointed at a table and pushed through the door into the restaurant. I brushed off the designated bench with my hand and then cleansed both of my hands with a sanitary wipe from my purse. I settled my already numb bottom on the hard wooden bench and sighed deeply.

Vaughn emerged with two plastic baskets lined with parchment paper. Nestled inside the paper were the biggest soft tacos I had ever seen. Neat bundles of flour tortilla wafting delicate tendrils of steam.

And I learned that I couldn't have been more wrong about Vaughn's palate.

"Good?" he asked when I came up for air and licked my fingers.

I could only groan with pleasure.

We were alone out in the sunshine because most people don't eat massive, debilitatingly delicious tacos in the middle of a weekday morning. However, I had no doubt the crowds would be arriving soon. I wished my stomach was bigger.

The timing wasn't fantastic, but I figured I might not get another shot at Vaughn's undivided attention—or nearly undivided since I was sharing it with only a magnificent taco. "So, not suicide?" I asked.

Vaughn quit chewing. "No," he said warily.

"You're sure?"

"Yes."

"How?"

"State secret. Unless you're the murderer. In which case, you tell me."

"I'm not the murderer."

"I know."

"But my client might be? Is that what you're saying?"

Vaughn frowned and wadded up his greasy napkin. "I already told you he has an alibi for most of that very large time window."

"*Most*," I muttered. I collected loose strands of shredded beef that had escaped from my taco and popped them into my mouth. "Not an accident either?"

Vaughn answered by flattening his brows into two straight lines. I took that as a no.

"What about the women?"

Vaughn has very acrobatic brows. Now they were perfect arches over his faintly amused brown eyes. "What do *you* know about them?"

I shrugged. "Not much. Just that there were a lot of them."

"Tell me about it." Vaughn sighed.

"So that's what you've been doing." I chuckled. "Interviewing a bunch of emotionally distraught and bereaved women. No wonder you needed sustenance."

"Not all of them are grieving Ian's passing," Vaughn admitted. "He tended to create a lot of animosity just before breaking up with them. Seemed to be a pattern." He collected my basket and stacked it with his own. "Caveat emptor."

I knew all about that.

CHAPTER 10

Vaughn dropped me off next to my ancient Volvo which was still complacently rusting away in the police department parking lot. Somebody could do me a great favor by stealing it, but I'd probably have to park it elsewhere to improve the odds of filing an insurance claim in the near future.

After a quick phone call to my sister, I set off on another round of errands, my trusty map once again gracing my lap. I'm old-school that way, the sole reason being that I am intimately familiar, due to my last job, with the nefarious purposes for which GPS can be used. There is no way I would willingly plug one of those devices into my car. Or use that feature on my phone, for that matter. I wouldn't mind if we all reverted to using the Pony Express, but I don't expect my views to be popular or practicable either.

Home improvement store, rental equipment place where I exchanged the pressure washer for a paint sprayer machine and the same clerk gave me the same degree of sparse instructions, and a little neighborhood grocery that specialized in fresh pasta. Since I owed Cal a lasagna soon,

I had to outsource that particular aspect of the process to someone else.

I chose the full porcini sheets so I—or rather, Willow—would be able to cut them to fit my pan, which absolutely delighted the proprietor. He wasn't sparse with his comments, and we ended up gabbing for close to half an hour in a very Italian way with lots of hand gesturing and free samples of his other products. It was all I could do to get out of the store without spending a hundred dollars, but it was also an inspiring experience.

How many navy-blue, beat-up Honda Accords were there in Portland? Probably a lot. The Accord is a popular car. In fact, I remembered seeing it on a list of the most frequently stolen vehicles in the United States. Alas, my Volvo had not been on the list.

But how many of the navy-blue Accords in Portland had a dent in the left front bumper and were burning enough oil to make visible chugs of smoke come out the exhaust pipe? And how many of them needed to go to the exact same places I was going and at the exact same times and in the exact same sequence as I was? It was a little disconcerting.

I kept peeking into the rearview mirror, but I couldn't see the driver clearly. He or she hadn't gotten out of the car or followed me around inside the stores. The car just seemed to always be there. Not tailgating, but following nonetheless. Patiently, too. The long-winded discourse on sauces and cured meats and cheeses at the grocery had proved that. Definitely creepy, but not threatening—yet.

I decided to hold my phone on my lap. Just in case a 911 call was in order.

I couldn't think of anywhere else to go. And I'd made arrangements to meet Sloane at the marina so we could get a jump on house painting while it was still sunny. So I headed for home, getting a crick in my neck while watching the movements of the car behind me.

When I slowed to pull into the marina's parking lot, the Accord sped up and zipped around me, too fast for me to handle the turn and imprint the driver's face on my memory at the same time. Gone—in a blur.

What silliness. I was being paranoid. But my chagrin didn't stop me from levitating off the seat when the phone in my lap rang.

"Eva?" Lila sounded breathless. "Do you have a few minutes?"

Sloane's minivan wasn't in the parking lot yet, so I said, "Sure. What's up?"

"Frank was just fabulous this morning," she gushed. "I wanted to let you know to watch the news tonight—all four of the network stations will be airing at least a portion of his interview. Good stuff." Lila sounded like a kid who'd just received a long-desired birthday gift. Performance is the currency of public relations, so I could understand her enthusiasm.

"Your talking points were perfect. Frank especially loved the trust fund idea. He's getting one of his friends to set up a trust for Ian's son. He can't have the Cox and Associates name associated with it, of course—you know how it is—but he'll see to it that it's accomplished." Lila carried on, providing a play-by-play recounting of the morning's media hour.

I scrunched the phone between my ear and shoulder and popped the trunk. I could haul and listen, probably. Maybe a headset would be a good investment, considering my new living situation.

Lila chattered ebulliently while I shuttled supplies to my house and trudged back for the next load. And the next. And the next. The girl was either ecstatic or in a nervous tizzy, and I didn't think Frank Cox's problems justified either emotional extreme.

"Whoa," I puffed as I leaned against the open door to the backseat of my car. I told myself I was just taking a breather before the final load. I interrupted her mid-sentence. "How long have you worked with Frank?"

"What?" Lila squeaked. "Oh, about two months."

"Is that all?" I was being sarcastic—public relations is a notoriously transient business.

But Lila answered with timid somberness. "Of course. But we haven't, you know—the other has been just recently. You won't tell, will you? I mean, I know it's not professional behavior to also have a romantic relationship with a client, but we're keeping it strictly separate."

How did I get into these things? Ugh. How, how, how???

For once, Lila was silent as though she expected feedback. Or perhaps exoneration.

"Let me guess," I muttered. "His alibi?"

"Me," Lila whimpered. "The detective asked, specifically, so I had to tell him, you know? But he promised to be discreet, no need for anyone to know except him—and well, now you."

Terrific. I must have the word *confidante* stamped on my forehead.

Gravel crunched as Sloane pulled her minivan in beside my Volvo. She flashed me a broad smile and a thumbs-up through the window. Which gave me a marvelous excuse to extricate myself from the call and shoot house painting to the top of my priority list.

While I made good-bye and good-luck noises— which took some time considering Lila's distraught condition—Sloane hopped out of her vehicle and pulled open the Volvo's other rear door. She scooped the remaining items off the backseat and helped me carry them down to the house.

"Client?" she asked once we'd dumped the last load and I'd clicked off the phone and set it on the kitchen counter with a scowl.

"Yep." I debated turning off the ringer, but figured I wouldn't be able to hear it anyway with the racket we'd soon be making. "What's that?" I pointed to a tattered manila folder she'd also placed on the counter.

"It was on the backseat of your car. Did you not want it brought down?"

"I don't know what it is." I flipped open the folder and was confronted with a sheaf of charts, graphs, and tiny font. Inside the front cover, someone had hastily scrawled a note—so hastily that I couldn't read the handwriting, even with considerable squinting.

"Time's a wastin'," Sloane warned cheerfully.

"Right." I tapped the folder and its contents into order and stacked it on my laptop, then I followed her out to the deck where the sprayer and gallons of *Grizzly*—a sort of brownish-gray, or was it grayish-brown?—paint awaited us. I should get that job, the naming of paint colors. Probably where the big bucks were. To my discriminating eye, the paint was the color of weathered cedar shake, which I considered quintessentially appropriate, if boring, for a floating house tethered at a marina. And certainly better than the current rusting aesthetic of the cargo containers.

Sloane has a knack for mechanical things, so she tackled setting up the paint sprayer while I slapped plastic sheets and tape all over the windows and doors and draped cloths over the deck. Then it was just a matter of gophering after her as she quickly and precisely swathed the sides of my house with paint. I made sure the line stayed unkinked and the tank was refilled immediately.

Communicating through the noise and activity was difficult, but we managed to catch up with each other in short spurts. The kids were having grandma time—with Riley's mother—so we could talk about grown-up stuff like jobs and shoes and tacos and the impropriety and inconvenience of other people's romantic flings.

"I don't get it." I finally voiced the bothersome idea that had been nagging at me since Lila's call. "What's the point? If Frank is covered and not a suspect in Ian's murder, and Lila knows this since she's his alibi, then why are they both so anxious about their—or really, his—reputation? Wouldn't it just be better for him to stay quiet, lie low for a while? They don't need me."

Sloane laughed and flicked the sprayer vertically along a narrow strip of metal at the corner of the house. "Sounds like you have yourself a sinecure."

"Sounds like you've been sneaking a peek at Roxy's word-a-day calendar." I snorted, but Sloane's observation was accurate. I had an easy, almost fluffy, job for which I had negotiated a hefty hourly fee. Show up a few times, make a few notes, listen to Lila's woes. From all appearances, that was the extent of what would be required of me.

"You're not complaining, are you?" Sloane asked.

"I guess not."

One of the joys of a small house is the modest exterior surface area, which Sloane and the speedy sprayer gobbled up. The transformation was remarkable; Sloane is the best company; and therefore, my mood improved accordingly. Amazing how that works.

Willow showed up as we were folding the drop cloths and swishing sprayer parts in buckets of clean water. If she noticed that I'd purchased the paint color she'd selected (from within my parameters), she didn't say so. But she was genial and didn't seem to be holding a grudge over our interrupted kayaking expedition the previous night.

"You on for lasagna tonight?" I asked.

She replied with a wide grin and a bob of her blue-hair topknot. Much better than the usual snorting.

The evening swelled into an even greater flurry of activity. Sloane waved good-bye so she could hurry home and clean up for a dinner date with Riley—they'd made detailed plans in order to take full advantage of Mrs. Tillman's babysitting prowess while it was available. Willow demonstrated an extraordinary ability to splatter tomato sauce on the fronts of my upper kitchen cabinets, the side of the refrigerator, the floor, and the oven door. But she handled the onion chopping with aplomb in spite of the eye-watering and sniffliness it engendered.

It wasn't until after the lasagna had been delivered to Cal and Willow had returned home to polish the play script she was developing from one of her space-opera stories which had a steampunk twist (I was still a little fuzzy on the plot details, although she had described her worldbuilding in depth) and I'd settled on the sofa in my richly-fragrant house (there's nothing like fresh lasagna to overpower the odor of fresh paint) with a mug of peppermint tea that I remembered the odd folder Sloane had found on the backseat of my car.

And the video clips of Frank's interviews which I'd promised Lila I would watch. I propped my laptop on my cross-legged lap to do that first. I don't have television, but the news channels' websites are just as good, and you don't have to endure so many ads.

Frank is a golden boy, in every way. Short sandy-brown hair, a healthy skin tone that indicated he might have freckled profusely in his youth, glistening straight teeth, candid blue eyes, and an easygoing manner. Not at all camera shy or awkward. I didn't know what Lila had been so worried about.

Three of the local stations played almost exactly the same cuts, just minor variations on a theme from slightly different vantage points. The fourth station played an even shorter clip which I assumed was the best of the best of the best, leaving all the *um*s and *ah*s and ear scratches and reporter microphone fumbles on the cutting-room floor. Through it all, Frank performed admirably as an upstanding businessman and concerned community member.

Check. I closed my laptop, shoved it away, and replaced it with the folder.

It took me about twenty minutes, but I ended up fairly confident in my final translation of the scratchy handwriting on the inside of the front flap: *Didn't mean to freak you out—if I did. Saw you taking notes at the press conference today. I'm taking a leap here, but I noticed you're cozy with that detective too. For Ian's sake, these reports need to get to the right people. Can I count on you? I can't keep them anymore and I can't take them to the police myself. You'll never hear from me again. P.S. Your passenger-side rear tire is a little squishy. Might want to get that fixed.*

Curiosity sufficiently piqued, I flipped through the pages. But it became clear that I would need something akin to a degree in biology or chemistry to understand them. *Hg* seemed to be a common notation, which required refamiliarizing myself with the periodic table of the elements to learn that it stood for mercury. Something called methylmercury was also mentioned. And it was pretty obvious that the levels of both were going up.

I had two calls to make. I chose the easier one first.

When Vaughn answered, I said, "When you searched Ian's apartment, did you find documents related to some kind of river water quality study?"

He was silent for a long time.

I stretched my legs out on the coffee table and wiggled my toes while I waited. I was in need of a pedicure. In my current financial situation, it would have to be a do-it-yourself-er, but I couldn't remember unpacking any nail polish.

Vaughn must have resolved his quandary, because he finally said, "I don't have the analysis back yet. A professor down at Oregon State University is taking a look at it for me."

"I either have a duplicate set of results or additional information," I said. "Would you be able to tell by looking? I could bring them to you."

"Eva," he sighed, "how on earth—? You know what, don't answer that. I'm coming to you. You have better coffee anyway." He hung up.

Which was exactly what I'd hoped for, because I so did not want to make the second phone call. Any excuse— even the excuse of having to confess the indiscretions of a stranger to a grouchy detective—to postpone making that call was fine with me.

CHAPTER 11

Vaughn must have exceeded the speed limit because he was knocking on my door in less than ten minutes. Or else he lived really close by—but that was a question I wasn't about to ask.

I'd spread the contents of the folder out on the kitchen bar and had the coffee ready to pour. Vaughn slid onto a barstool and hunched over the papers, elbows planted on the countertop and chin cupped in his hands.

I left him in peace. I mean figuratively, not literally. I stood quietly on the kitchen side of the bar and tried really hard not to fidget while he systematically absorbed the printed information.

He lingered over the hand-scrawled note and my penciled transcription beside it.

He finally took a break to gulp his coffee. "Okay," he said, "where and how?"

"This afternoon. I think I was followed from the police department parking lot, but the first time I really noticed was when I left Home Depot. It was a navy-blue Honda Accord. I never got a good look at the driver. When I arrived here, the Accord sped past, but I assume he or she doubled back and slipped the folder into my car while I wasn't looking."

"You left your car unlocked?"

I nodded. "And wide open. I had to make a lot of trips. Stuff—you know."

"You painted." Vaughn sniffed and glugged the rest of his coffee. "Looks good."

I swung into action to refill his mug. "It's dark outside and the paint's gray. There's not much to see at the moment. But I'll trust your deduction skills, Sherlock, and accept the compliment on my sister's behalf. What about the documents? Look familiar?"

"A couple of them. The rest are different. I'll pass these along to Dr. Ramsay as well. Frankly, they look older—the dates..." He dove into a renewed examination and shuffling. He seemed to be arranging the pages chronologically. "But this"—Vaughn stabbed a forefinger on the informant's note—"is especially interesting."

"Agreed. A sort of Good Samaritan stalker, I guess. I think it sounds like a woman. Would a man tell me about my squishy tire like that?"

"If he got a good look at you—which he did if he followed you through multiple shopping sprees—then, yes, he most likely would." Vaughn shrugged. "I know I would."

"My purchases were all necessities. Absolutely. Every one of them," I groused. Then I pointed an emphatic finger at his chest. "You're assuming he's a nice guy. Like you," I added with a smirk.

But my humor was lost on Vaughn. "Pays attentions to details, I'll give him that." He shook his head and scooped the papers back into the folder. "This research—the frequency of the observations—required a lot of dedication."

"So, um..." I bit my lip. It was a sensitive subject, but *ethics* demanded that I bring it up. "Frank's alibi. I know about that too."

For the first time that evening, Vaughn's little tilted smile made an appearance. "I figured you would, sooner or later. Girls talk, right?"

My mouth was open for some kind of snappy, gender-bias-crushing retort—I don't know which one, exactly—but Vaughn stood as if he was suddenly in a hurry.

"Walk me out to my truck. Bring a flashlight."

"Why? Are you scared of the dark?" I snickered, proving just how far into juvenile snarkiness I can sink.

"I'm going to change your tire," he said sensibly. And kindly.

I immediately deflated. "Oh. Thank you."

"Consider it repayment for dinner last night."

Right. No favors.

Our footsteps reverberated along the floating walkway, making it bounce in little skooshy slaps against the water's surface. Otherwise, the night was quiet. The porthole in the cabin of Cal's sailboat was a black circle. I hoped he hadn't gorged so much on the lasagna that he'd made himself ill.

I wished it was daylight, because I would have liked to watch Vaughn scrounging around in the gravel, wrestling with my tire, but I couldn't catch very much of the rest of his body in my flashlight beam as I concentrated on aiming it at his hands. However, it was clear he'd done this sort of thing before.

Fortunately, the spare tire in the trunk was sufficiently inflated. I couldn't remember the last time I'd checked on its condition—probably never. Vaughn finished the operation with an economy of words, climbed into his truck, and drove off with the mysterious scientific folder tucked safely on the seat beside him.

As I trudged back toward the gangplank, I spotted the solitary orange glow of the burning end of a cigarette create a quarter-circle arc as the smoker holding it lifted it to her lips.

"He's sure paying you a lot of attention," Roxy said softly once the arc had been reversed. She followed the comment with a concentrated, audible exhale.

I veered in her direction. She was a darker lump in front of the darkened office building. I presumed she was sitting on the bench just outside the office door.

I found the bench by banging my knee on it, and I plopped down beside her. "Purely of a professional nature," I asserted. "But Chief Monk specifically requested that I pass along his *best* regards to you."

"Did he now?" Although I couldn't see her face clearly, it sounded as though Roxy was smiling. Another deep inhale and the ember at the end of her cigarette flared. "We've had our moments."

"Not all of them sounded pleasant from his report. Body watching? Why didn't you tell me it was a common occurrence here at the marina?"

Roxy's clothing rustled, accompanying what was probably a shrug. Her weight shifted on the bench. "It's not the sort of thing one puts in brochures advertising a bucolic life on the river. Besides, it depends on your definition of common. Certainly not so frequently as to be bromidic. Four, five—maybe six. But I've been here for going on thirty years. This one was Willow's first, though."

I made a mental note to look up *bucolic* and *bromidic* when I got back to the house. Yet another demonstration of the value of keeping a word-a-day calendar in one's office. I should take up the habit.

"Is she doing okay?" I asked.

"Far as I can tell. Keeps herself busy. She writes those disturbing fantasy stories anyway—has since she was about ten years old. Maybe that's how she copes with all the frustration and anxiety that's bottled up inside her. Her life's certainly not been easy, poor kid." Another deep inhale. Roxy savored her cigarettes, extracting every last carcinogenic molecule out of them.

"Did you know I took your advice?" I ventured. "I spread my business cards around Portland City Hall and got a job out of it. Public relations for Frank Cox." I held my breath, waiting for her reaction.

While her tone was mild, she didn't bother to hide the edge of disgust in her voice. "The great finagler."

"Did you encounter him at the community meeting about the development on the other side of the wildlife refuge?"

Roxy flicked her lighter to life, illuminating her opposite hand and a new cigarette nestled above the still-burning stub between her fingers. Apparently, her opinion of Frank Cox necessitated even more nicotine than usual.

"I did," she replied once her lungs were smoke-filled. "Smarmy devil. In cahoots with Ross Perkins—the city commissioner—if you ask me."

I'd been hesitant to broach that extended subject, so I was glad she'd volunteered. "I was afraid of that," I whispered. "It's all been a little too good to be true. But the development isn't inside Portland city limits. In fact, it's not in any city, just in unincorporated Multnomah County."

"Ah, but Cox owns plenty of buildings and land inside Portland too. He has holdings all over the metro area, out to Hillsboro and Beaverton, plus over on the eastern side of the state in Bend. The guy's a magnate of

Oregon real estate. He makes sure he gets what he wants by buddying up with politicians of all stripes and locales. I suppose you could say he grooms them in case he ever needs favors down the road."

Roxy's information made the phone call I'd been postponing that much easier. In fact, I was now desperate to place it, regardless of how badly I needed an income.

~oOo~

It was awfully late, but Lila and I had already held several conversations well outside conventional business hours. Most of which had also included, at Lila's instigation, *girl talk,* as Vaughn had so derogatorily termed it. So without any pang to my sense of propriety, I punched in her number.

But I got her voice mail. I had no idea how long it would let me babble. I should have written my own talking points before dialing, but that would have required delaying for a few minutes, and I couldn't wait to quit.

Lila deserved an explanation, though, concerning my ethical qualms about the man she was probably cozied up with at that very moment. So I just said, in general terms, that some things had come to my attention regarding Cox and Associates and that the information presented a conflict of interest for me. Besides, I added, she seemed entirely competent in the realm of public relations, and my services were redundant anyway. That way, I appealed to her across the spectrum—practically (i.e. economically), professionally, and personally. A successful argument. And all before the voice mail service cut me off.

Duty completed, I still knew I wouldn't be sleeping anytime soon. So I launched into the only reasonable substitute—hanging curtains.

All the lights were blazing in the loft because I needed to see what I was doing. But it also meant that anyone in the marina who was curious and awake at that late hour could also observe the adventure I was embarking upon. I was operating under the assumption that living in the public eye would have to get worse before it could get better. But if I worked fast...

Up, down, shove the ladder over two feet, up, down, with eyebolts clamped between my lips and cable and pipe sections pinned under my arms. Sloane had brought over Riley's electric drill with some handy attachments that made the repetitive task somewhat easier.

Willow's vision of hanging fabric panels to separate functional spaces in the loft was brilliant. Open, close, look out the expansive windows, or not—I'd be able to shift the curtains around at will for whatever level of privacy and view I wanted, not to mention controlling the degree of sun glare streaming in if I was working at my desk.

The arrangements were finally completed to my satisfaction in the wee hours of the morning. I'd also discovered muscles in my arms that I'd neglected for far too long, and they screamed for relief. I tugged several curtain panels into a cozy cocoon around my bed, kicked my shoes off, and slid under the duvet, fully clothed and unwashed.

~oOo~

Which is an unpleasant way to awaken. My mouth was fuzzy and my eyelids felt glued together. But somewhere in the not-too-distant reaches a phone was chiming "You Are My Sunshine" most obnoxiously.

I found it on the rug beside my shoes. Apparently, it had become a lumpy nuisance in the night, and I'd removed it from my pocket and banished it to the floor as well. The caller ID said Lila Halton. I groaned and flopped back on the bed. I certainly wasn't at the top of my form at the moment, nor was I prepared to deal with anger or resentment or recriminations.

I gritted my teeth. "Good morning."

"Eva, I totally understand," Lila said.

Which made me sit up and rub my eyes fully open. "Really?"

"Of course. I'll cut your check today. Frank just likes to cover all his bases, but he agrees that maybe this PR blitz has been overkill, especially since Detective Malloy called and asked to meet with Frank in an hour. Who knows, maybe the case has been resolved." There was a forced cheerfulness to her tone, as though she was trying to convince herself of the truth of her own words.

I had no desire to dash her hopes, even though I had a pretty good idea what Vaughn wanted to question Frank about. "Thanks, Lila. Look, if you ever have any other clients, I'd love to work with you again. It's been a pleasure." Not to mention easy. But always good to leave things on a positive note.

"Oh sure," she gushed. "Frank's taking all my time right now, but yes, of course. So um..." A faint rustling sounded as though she'd switched the phone to her other ear. "I heard—Eva, was one of your conflicts that you found the body?"

I dropped back among the pillows again and squinted at the ceiling. "Not really. At least not at the time. I considered Ian and Frank completely separate, uh, situations. Until—that is…"

Talk about a conflict—here it was staring me in the face, and waiting none-too-patiently on the phone. Think, think, think—quickly. Vaughn needed to be able to handle the questioning of Frank in his own way and with the degree of surprise he judged appropriate. I was certain that whatever I said to Lila would get passed on to Frank immediately.

But Lila, who had never been comfortable with gaps in conversation, rushed on and gave me a reprieve. "How was he?" She breathed raggedly into the phone.

I rolled over and snaked an arm out to wiggle a gap in the curtains. Another gorgeous day. But apparently it wasn't lending any more clarity to Lila's thinking process than it was to mine.

"How was who?" I asked.

"Ian. When you found him."

I blinked in the sliver of bright sunshine streaking through the crack in the curtains. What kind of question was that? *Predominantly dead* would be the correct answer, but could I say that out loud? If she had to ask, then what kind of answer could she possibly be hoping for?

I decided on, "Submerged. I couldn't see him very well. Just enough to—well, I didn't know who it was until later, and since I'd never met him—"

"Right, right," Lila murmured. "Yes, sorry. Gosh. That must have been terrible. It's just that when the police said he was unconscious before he drowned…"

The medical examiner had said that, actually—not Chief Monk. But I didn't bother to correct her. "Did you know Ian well?" I asked instead.

"What? Oh. Yeah. He was very active—environmentally, politically, you know. I think everyone in certain circles couldn't help but know him." She laughed—a sort of forced jollity.

And perhaps he also was exceptionally familiar with everyone female, since he had reportedly been a perpetual dater. I knew from experience that that kind of awareness went both ways, much like how Doc was warned about but marginally tolerated by the double-X chromosome contingent within the marina.

Because, no matter what Vaughn's opinion was, I couldn't get over the impression that my stalker/informant of the previous day had been a woman. Beyond the helpful notice about the squishy tire, I suspected my hunch was connected to the use of the word *cozy*, where the writer had suggested that I was cozy with Vaughn. I was pretty sure a man wouldn't have described that observation with such an emotive term.

But did it matter? So Ian had known a lot of women, and a lot of women had known Ian. Surely Frank Cox wasn't the only male in the suspect pool?

I sighed, grateful that it was Vaughn's problem and not mine. "Well, take care," I said to Lila.

"Back atcha," she returned cheerfully.

CHAPTER 12

Bolstered by the feeling of an incredible lightness of being, otherwise known as a freshly-relieved conscience, I pulled on my grubbiest clothes and headed straight outside for a day of trim painting. A shower could wait—indefinitely. Sloane had warned me about the prolonged and incessant rainy season in the Pacific Northwest. I figured the clock was ticking on the stretch of good weather we'd been enjoying.

Painting is good for sorting thoughts, too. I was trying to categorize each of the swirling suspicions in my head and consign them to their respective buckets so that I could focus. My one remaining client was going to need my undivided attention, and soon.

And that's when it happened. Blam! The best idea in the past forty-eight hours. I dashed up to the loft office, made a few phone calls, manipulated a couple design files, canceled an order in the barest nick of time, created a new order, and returned to the great outdoors breathless but happy.

Brilliant. Sometimes I surprise myself. Which just goes to show how much the Frank Cox/Ian Thorpe ethical dilemma had been bogging me down. So totally worth it to "fire" a client and free up those brain cells.

But I was in for another surprise—Cal had taken my place. He held the narrow angle brush delicately in his thin, long-fingered hand, as though it was a set of ivory chopsticks, and he was perched on the step stool, applying an even coat of white paint to the top sash of my kitchen window. The poor guy must be ravenous.

The least I could do was keep him company.

"You've done this before," I said, admiring the perfectly straight line he was producing without apparent effort. In spite of his ragged physical condition, his nerves were steadier than mine.

Cal offered a wan smile over his shoulder. "Your door was unlocked, so I slipped the brownie pan inside. I'm still working on the lasagna."

What was it with open doors and the irresistible impulse to *slip something through them* in this place? The opposite of pack-rat-ism? Neighborly generosity? Or plain old nosiness? I had the feeling it would be futile to complain.

"The curtains are a nice touch," Cal added.

Yeah, so he couldn't watch me sleeping anymore. Although, nothing about Cal set off my self-defense radar. I figured he'd be the last voyeur I'd ever have to worry about. In fact, his voyeurism—if that's what it really was—seemed to have a purpose. A purpose worth exploring.

"You're like the silent sentry of the marina," I said. "Or a guardian angel. Old habit?"

Cal shrugged, somehow maintaining a smooth flow of paint from the brush while his shoulders rose and returned to their loose perpendicular line. "I suppose. Instinct."

"Training?" I countered.

Another shrug.

"Which only reinforced a natural inclination." I was stream-of-consciousness talking, musing about the sort of genetics and upbringing that would incline a young boy to grow into a successful CIA covert operative, if, indeed, the rumors about Cal were true.

The shrewd glance Cal darted my direction indicated I was hitting close to the mark—or maybe it was just my romanticized imagination running away with me.

"Spear phishing?" Cal muttered.

I grinned. So I had been in the right territory. "Guilty," I replied.

"Quit?"

"Laid off."

"Left hanging out to dry." Cal's tone was flat—it was a statement, not a question. I suspected he'd experienced something similar. It's not an uncommon event for those who work in certain arenas—the embarrassing ones the federal government is occasionally forced to acknowledge publicly due to some kind of screwup.

I grunted in agreement.

"This is a good place to settle." Cal kicked the step stool over and started on the bathroom window frame.

I followed cautiously. I didn't want to crowd him, so I plopped down on the deck, rolled up my pant legs and dangled my feet in the river. Casual, right?

"This deal with Ian Thorpe," I said. "I'm curious."

"That's reasonable."

I almost chucked aloud. There was a flow to Cal's words just as there was a flow of paint from his brush. But the words weren't nearly as smooth. Herky-jerky, but not unwilling.

So I started slowly. "Had you seen him out kayaking before?"

"Twice a week. Work, not pleasure."

In my vast experience with kayaking, it had been *both* work and pleasure. "How can you tell the difference?"

"Timing. No one who's doing it for pleasure keeps such a regular schedule."

"Was he collecting water samples?" I asked.

This earned me another shrewd glance. "His technology was more sophisticated than that. He installed sensors at various points in the current."

Wow. Cal had moved from spurts of information to a deluge in a matter of seconds. I struggled to fully grasp the meaning of Ian's regular activities. "Did you ever get a good look at his equipment?"

Cal emitted the softest snort—in no way approaching Willow's expressive territory—but it made me realize I'd asked a dumb question. So I doubled up. "Were the sensors enabled for active signaling or just passive data collection?"

"You coming around the corner?" Cal asked.

I scrabbled after him as he moved on to paint the trim around the French doors leading from the empty bedroom on the other side of the house.

But he didn't need additional prompting. He answered so rapidly that I thought he'd been mulling over these particular details for a while. "Active, but they're fragile, and it seems they got clogged or became erratic on a regular basis, which is why Ian had to go out and check them twice a week. There was a threshold above which each unit would produce an alarm signal—not audible, but an additional alert to the receiving unit, wherever Ian had that located."

"What was he measuring?"

"Unknown. But I can guess. The Willamette's had problems with mercury for a long time. Basin runoff mostly. But that goes back to whatever airborne pollutants we have. Pervasive, really."

"So why is it an issue now?"

Cal shook his head. "The river's been somewhat cleaned up. Enough so that the health department has issued mild encouragement regarding the safety of eating fish caught in the river—provided you don't eat too many of them, of course." He squatted to neatly apply paint to the lower trim. "Considering that it was a pet project of Ian's, it's one of two things. Either there's been a recent increase in river pollution overall or the pollution already in the river has built to a point that it's harming other species that call the place home. River otters come to mind. They're an indicator species because they primarily feed on fish. A pollutant like mercury accumulates as it advances through the food chain."

I'd heard the warnings, of course, about fish like tuna and swordfish. Particularly that pregnant women shouldn't eat such delicacies. It was the sort of factoid that rattled around in the back of my head but which I'd paid little attention to since my tuna sandwiches were few and far between.

"How many people knew Ian was collecting this data?" I asked aloud. Not that I expected Cal to have an answer.

"More than one, I'm guessing." His bright blue eyes glinted, as though he knew exactly what had been dropped on the backseat of my car the day before.

I wondered if Ian had intentionally spread the data around for safekeeping. I also wondered if that was what had gotten him killed.

~oOo~

Friday was hectic but in the best possible sense. Filled to the brim with the kind of frantic errands, perfecting touches, and petty anxieties that make the work of marketing so challenging and so fun.

The *Willamette Week* reporter had been eager to do a write-up about the Wicked Bean Annex, so I had a meeting scheduled with her and Darren in the morning. On the way, I stopped at the printer—the amazing, flexible, last-minute printer that had swapped orders for me and was now permanently engraved in my list of reliable contacts—to pick up the coasters, coffee cup sleeves, and matchbooks inked with the Annex's snazzy new logo. There is absolutely nothing better than making swag functional in order to extend its marketing life, especially if the promotional item is also reusable and collectible.

The reporter presented an image, poignantly, of what Willow might look like in another decade—perky, inquisitive, tattooed (which, I think, helped alleviate Darren's pretty bad case of nerves about being interviewed), pierced in so many visible places that I shuddered to think what she'd done to the body parts I couldn't see, and dazzlingly intelligent. Whip smart. A million questions a minute with laughs in between.

Her name was Josie Rodriguez, and she had magenta and black streaked hair with an extra white streak along the left side of her face. Remarkable. I had a hard time keeping my staring to a minimum.

If Darren had been overwhelmed by my enthusiasm for his new venture earlier, then facing Josie ratcheted everything up exponentially. He walked around the cavernous room—which now had café tables and chairs and rolling partitions that could be hung with artwork and positioned for strategic viewing enclaves—trailing Josie with his hands stuffed in his pockets and a mesmerized half-grin on his face, but he managed to lucidly answer the questions she fired at him. I only interrupted when I thought he was being too humble.

When Josie had collected more than enough material and was finished oohing and ahhing, I walked out to her car with her.

"Thanks so much for doing a feature," I said.

"Couldn't resist. I have so many friends who will be clamoring for studio space in there. Can you imagine? It's everything you need—coffee, music, like-minded companions sitting right next to you to gossip with, and a setup for doing your art, if you can find the time with all the distractions." She chortled. "Half of art is talking about it, anyway, for most of us. Pondering. It's the angst thing."

"So, uh, placement? And the article will come out on Wednesday?" I asked, ever mindful of my client. He needed her glowing review to appear before his official grand opening the following weekend.

Josie made a face. "This thing with Ian—the murder? It's crowding my column. That shouldn't happen, you know? Murder, politics, all that droll stuff—they get the entire news section. Should be plenty of space, and I'm squarely in the arts and entertainment section. But leads are pouring in left and right, speculation up the wazoo, conspiracy theories, you name it. I feel bad for our news reporters who are chasing down all the wacko tipsters and trying to make sense of it all before the deadline." She sighed. "I'll do what I can. I got the photos you emailed. Good pics always help win a place in my editor's heart and inches on the page."

So Josie was on a first-name basis with Ian Thorpe too? Not surprising, I supposed, considering what I'd learned in the past few days. I couldn't help myself—I had to ask. "So what's the prevailing theory? At the moment?"

"Seriously? Three-quarters of the people on our staff, including the advertising manager—who's supposed to be happy taking anyone's money, right? No biases?— think Ross Perkins had something to do with it. You'd never catch that guy actually in a kayak—it'd sink—and visualizing him enjoying nature from the bank of the river is an enormous stretch too—so placing him at the scene, wherever that is, requires quite a suspension of disbelief. But it feels grimy, which is pretty typical of Ross's dealings. Something underhanded, a bribe, a kickback, a weekend at a spa in Sonoma for his wife, that kind of stuff. He always pays up when he gets caught, is really good at the 'It was a simple misunderstanding' line. Murder would be new for him, but it's probably the next logical thing on his list."

Josie ticked the city commissioner's alleged crimes off on her fingers. "Bribery, influence peddling, extortion, nepotism, cronyism, adultery, fooling around with a girl who was a few weeks shy of her eighteenth birthday, theft, larceny. Yeah, if he wants to get creative, I guess murder's the next step."

"And yet he keeps getting reelected?" I blurted.

"Yeah, well, he's never been convicted. Whenever something comes up, he complains vociferously about people not understanding what it takes to be an effective politician, to do his constituents' work, et cetera. Says everything is complicated, points at his track record— which is rather full of progress if you measure progress by infrastructure and employment rates—and lays money on the table to cover his oversights. Probably his favorite term—*simple oversights*. Plural, mind you, *multiple* simple oversights. But he certainly gets things done, does our Ross."

I was left breathless just listening to Josie. No wonder Ross Perkins seemed to incite a visceral reaction from people—me, Roxy, Josie herself, and doubtless countless others. I wondered how far the news reporters would go in suggesting his complicity in Ian Thorpe's murder without actual evidence. Probably depended on how badly the publisher of the *Willamette Week* wanted to get sued.

~oOo~

I swapped the whirlwind that is Josie Rodriguez for the rubber-scented respite of the Les Schwab Tire Center waiting area. Vaughn had told me exactly where to go, with the added helpful tidbit that the friendly technicians would probably not charge me for repairing my flat tire even though I had never been a customer previously. This policy was designed to make people happy and encourage future purchases, and I dearly appreciated it.

I munched fresh (free!) popcorn and tried not to watch the muted true-crime reenactment television show that was playing on the flat screen mounted above a display of car batteries. I had enough true crime in my life as it was.

Instead, I tuned in to the conversation two old men were having on the other side of a dusty fake ficus tree that had been staked in a big wicker basket as a homey touch in the otherwise strictly utilitarian space.

Old Man #1, in a gray billed cap with a patch bearing the cursive word *Coastal* in a red oval stuck on the front, said, "You know that fellow got himself killed? Environmentalist? He came in my shop last week. Wanted rubberized tubing in a few different diameters. I think he was rigging up some kind of contraption to tow behind a boat."

"Could be, Marv," Old Man #2, the one in the green quilted down vest, said. "You seen those algae slicks on the banks? Getting worse. No way I'm dipping this pretty hide of mine in that water anytime soon. And those kids out there waterskiing. Probably get sick two days later and think nothing of it."

"Yep," Marv agreed. "Every time it rains, Portland flushes, and we get their sewage down here in Fidelity and points beyond."

The receptionist called Marv to the counter so he could pay for his wheel alignment, cutting off my chance at eavesdropping on more tantalizing details. On the television screen, the actress whom I assumed was playing the victim strolled through a stand of yellow-leafed trees, swinging her arms, blissfully unaware of the stranger in the blue hoodie crouched behind some bushes.

Ugh. I stood up, walked three feet, and plopped into a chair facing the other direction. No matter where I was—in the tiny town of Fidelity or in bustling Portland— it seemed everyone was buzzing about Ian Thorpe's murder. I supposed I'd missed out on the pervasiveness of the early hubbub since I didn't watch the local news or read the newspapers and I definitely didn't give any credence to the talking mediaheads who rehashed the few known details ad nauseam. But now that the case had spread to the point that it infiltrated dialogue among friends, I felt for Vaughn.

As a small-town police detective investigating the murder of a prominent activist, he had a tough job to do, with everyone watching. A little grouchiness was permissible.

CHAPTER 13

At what time would a spry older lady serve dinner to her new man friend? I was betting on six o'clock. A more formal affair would normally be scheduled for later in the evening, but if Norman was going to review Bettina's investment portfolio, I figured they'd want to get an early start.

I estimated an hour to enjoy the meal. If he was a gentleman, perhaps Norman would help with the dishes, occupying another half hour. So that put the financial discussion at seven-thirty—right around sunset. Perfect.

It was warm enough; I just had to hope that Bettina would have some of her windows open. It'd be disastrous to my plans if they sat out on the deck to talk, but I was counting on the perpetual river breeze to prompt them to stay inside since they'd probably be looking over a lot of papers.

I got everything ready: kayak, life jacket, paddle, binoculars, miniature digital audio recorder I still had from my college days, fresh batteries for the recorder, and my house key attached to a little block of foam on a chain around my neck. Check, check, check. I couldn't approach on the floating walkways since they were reverberating soundboards, announcing the arrival of all interlopers well in advance, so my only option was to sidle up next to Bettina's house by water.

I was sorely tempted to request Willow's assistance since my kayak-handling skills weren't up to par yet. But the kid deserved a Friday night without adult worries.

Even though my preparations reminded me of one of my favorite childhood books, *Harriet the Spy*, I had only a hint of vague uneasiness about what I was planning to do. And those misgivings were completely put to rest when I justified the operation by telling myself that I was doing it for Vaughn. I was certain he would want to make sure his mother was okay, and since he was so busy...and since he wasn't supposed to have learned about Bettina's latest heartthrob, at least not from me, given the sworn-to-secrecy thing...well, it was my unadulterated responsibility to scope out Norman, right?

Right. Yes, absolutely. I wound my hair into a low, floppy bun and pulled a brimmed cap down low over my eyes. Just another random kayaker, out enjoying nature.

Reflections from the walkway lampposts were squiggling in serpentine lines across the river's surface, and the first few stars were winking in the east. The high berm on the river's west side made sunset come just a few minutes earlier—minutes I put to use by tipping the kayak into the water, settling my long legs and fanny into the cockpit, and making myself comfortable. I had no idea how long I'd need to hang around under Bettina's windows, and I couldn't afford to have a muscle cramp cut my spying session short.

I wedged the audio recorder—safely encased in a Ziploc plastic bag—between my legs for easy access and zipped my life jacket up to my chin. Then I grabbed my paddle off the dock and released my line. Away!

It was so easy. Too easy, almost. I practiced dipping my paddle as quietly as possible—no flicks, splooshes, or weird cupping bubble sounds. Nice and easy. And slow. No rush.

Bettina's house was on the end of the E row on the far north side of the marina. So basically in line with my house, but I would have to cross the intervening B, C, and D rows. But the marina was blessedly quiet. The residents seemed to be either out for the evening or already settled inside for the night. No loud talking, smells of barbecue grills, clinks of glasses being refilled, or the putter of small engines returning from a day of exploring. Pretty unusual for a Friday night, but I'm in the habit of taking good luck when it comes around.

Bettina's house was lit up like the Fourth of July. All the windows and the sliding glass door to her deck glowed cheerily, and she had strings of colored lights strung all over her deck on the river side. My good luck continued in that most of her windows were open. Plus, her wind chimes were clanking dissonantly and steadily. I no longer had to worry about how much noise I might be making.

While the wind chimes provided terrific cover, they also made it impossible to hear any snips of conversation through the open windows. I couldn't even tell which room Bettina and her guest were in.

I slowly paddled around the three sides of the house that I could reach by water, ducking down when I crossed in front of a window. The kitchen window was too high to see into from my vantage point, except to know that they'd at least finished washing up at the sink. The dining room had no human occupants, but there was a large vase of African daisies centered on the table. I wondered if they'd been a gift from Norman.

Through the sliding glass door, I could see half the couch, half the coffee table and one recliner in Bettina's living room. All empty. The living room's large picture window revealed the other half of the couch and a second recliner. Again, no people.

I maneuvered the kayak around the corner and alongside the narrow strip that served as Bettina's front porch. That door was closed, and the louvers on the shutters that covered the accompanying window were angled in such a way that I couldn't see inside from down at water level.

Craning my neck, I could just peer down the land side of Bettina's house, and noted that the light in the bathroom was on. They couldn't both be in there, could they? Or maybe Norman had bailed early—that would be a relief. Or he'd gotten sick. Or Bettina had taken my advice and pretended to fall ill herself. All excellent possible outcomes.

I swung the kayak around, intending to make a second tour before calling it a night. The bedroom was on the far corner, and in the name of due diligence, I did need to try to get a peek in that window as well before my conscience could be considered clear on the matter.

Just as I was rounding the corner to the long, river-facing side of Bettina's house, the sliding door opened, and a tall man dressed in jeans and a pale-blue polo shirt stepped out onto the deck. I gasped and collapsed in half, face planted into my knees, the shaft of the paddle digging into my waist. The only possible way I could go without being seen was to become suddenly much, much smaller. Without guidance, my kayak started bobbing like a lost cork and bumping into the edge of the deck. I blindly stretched out a hand and tried to shove off—gently, not hard enough to attract attention.

And that's when the rest of the massive wake hit me. I'd seen the tug go by, pushing a flotilla of four barges, but that had been, what, twenty minutes ago? Fifteen? Ten? I'd completely forgotten about the delayed reaction of wakes and of how big they were when that much tonnage was moving through the water.

I tipped over in an instant. One moment, excruciatingly uncomfortable but dry; the next, cold, soaked through, and tangled up in my equipment, with gritty water in my mouth. The life jacket thrust me to the surface and forced an awkwardly angled list to all my movements.

No splashing, the eerie, woodenly calm, and practical voice in my head demanded. She sounded like a robot, this girl who took charge, but at least she wasn't talking out loud. She couldn't, because I had the zippered edge of the plastic bag containing the audio recorder clenched in my teeth. I must have made a reflexive movement to shove it there—to free my hands for treading water and to save my old college backup device which wasn't worth more than the batteries inside it at this point.

Terrific. I clung to a slender baluster—part of the railing that bordered Bettina's deck—and took further stock.

No paddle—it was completely gone. My kayak was riding the wake in toward shore—a dark blob on the dark surface of the water about twenty feet away.

"It's a limited time offer, darling," Norman said. "I can only guarantee returns greater than twenty percent to those who invest within the next month. You know how it is. These things go up and down, but right now they're going up."

Now that I was in the water, my head was below the level of the deck. I couldn't see them. If they had cared to look toward the sound of a hastily stifled splutter through clenched teeth, they would have seen four white fingers wrapped around a railing support post.

Bettina's answer was short and muffled. But there were thumps and then light tinkling sounds as though someone was swirling a teaspoon around inside a fine china teacup. The noise could have come from a wind chime—but it would have been a well-mannered and proper wind chime, which didn't really match my experience with Bettina's eclectic collection so far.

Whatever she'd said hadn't deterred him, because Norman carried on. "An opportunity of a lifetime, returns like this. And you can rest assured the fund is under good management. Any profits in excess of twenty percent will be reinvested, so you end up earning twenty percent of a growing pie. The bigger the pie, the bigger the slices, better for everyone."

Better for everyone, my ass—not to put too fine a point on it. Rats, rats, rats. My options at the moment were rather limited, and my body was quickly stiffening, turning into leaden, immobile weight. Whatever the air temperature was, the river felt at least thirty degrees colder.

"Well, it's certainly appealing," Bettina piped. "A chain of restaurants, you said? Aren't those kind of hit or miss?"

"Not these," Norman huffed. "Location is everything. Surely you've heard that. Location, location, location. Our restaurants will be perfectly situated in rapidly growing suburbs, where families will eat on their way home after a long day, and where they'll spend their weekends because they don't want to face the long drive into the city again. We'll have a captive clientele."

I just about choked again, but instead I tore the bag from my teeth, pinned it against the front of my life jacket and pried it open with my free hand. I let the bag slip away as yet another piece of human-negligent litter in the river, and carefully held the recorder up out of the water while I pressed the start button.

I slid the recorder behind the baluster closest to the wall of Bettina's house and propped it against the cedar shake siding. Just a small black box deep in the shadows. It would run until the batteries wore out, and I would have to figure out a way to retrieve it later.

I can swim. But it would be a long distance, in the dark, in a frigid and dirty river. Besides, I was shivering so hard, I didn't have full control of my limbs.

Bettina and Norman were still talking. Well, Norman was talking, and Bettina was making encouraging sounds at appropriate intervals.

My brain was too cold to listen anymore. I forced the fingers on my left hand to release the baluster, and I slowly, hand-over-hand, dragged myself along the edge of Bettina's deck. Past her front door, and across the width of the shallow front porch below the clanging wind chimes and through the orb of light from the lantern beside her door. I couldn't feel my fingers, my toes—all of my legs, really. Numb beyond description.

I was having a hard time keeping my eyes open. Which is why I didn't notice right away that someone had hold of my wrists—both of them.

CHAPTER 14

"I'm not spying," I murmured. "Not really. It's not what it looks like." And then I was lying face-first on the walkway. Someone was swinging my lower half up and out of the water too. My life jacket was a dripping heap a few feet away.

"Shhh," he whispered. "You're doing fine." Then he was taking off my sandals and rubbing my feet. "You're going to have to walk out of here, okay? Wiggle your toes."

I tried. I really did. But whatever movement I was able to conjure apparently wasn't impressive. He rubbed with renewed vigor.

Eventually, I sat up. "Okay," I croaked.

"Good." Cal grinned at me from where he was kneeling by my feet.

Not that I wanted him to stop or anything, because the way he was pressing his thumb into my arch was heavenly, but I thought some words were in order. "How did you—" I started, but Cal held up a warning finger.

He glanced over his shoulder at Bettina's brightly-lit house. "Let's get you out of here first, then we'll talk. I think Norman's wrapping up his spiel."

Cal levered me upright and wrapped a sinewy arm around my waist. As though we were playing a slow and ungainly game of Simon Says, he showed me—by feel as much as by sight—how to tread silently on the floating walkway. Which explained why he always seemed to be barefoot.

He'd collected my sandals and life jacket in his other hand, and they made soft splatty sounds as they dripped beside us. We had to take the long route—up the E walkway, along the main linking walkway to the locked gate, through the gate, along the rest of the main walkway to the A walkway.

"In here," Cal murmured. "It's better if the lights in your house don't come on just yet. We left a big wet spot and footprints on Bettina's walkway. She's not the suspecting sort, but Norman could be." He guided me to secure footing on the deck of his sailboat and opened the cabin door, which was just as silent as he was. The man must keep a fifty-gallon drum of WD-40 onboard.

He put a hand on the top of my head to show me how low to duck, and I scrabbled over the threshold and collapsed on something soft and cushiony inside. I could feel Cal moving about in the darkness behind me and the air pressure change when he closed the cabin door. Then a match flared, illuminating his face while he lit an old-fashioned oil lamp.

"Open flame," I murmured.

"In the hands of a responsible person and owner of this boat." Cal emitted a subdued chuckle at his minor infraction of the marina rules. "They're technically illegal, all Roxy's precautions. I'm in my own domain here, not on marina property. I guess if I want to burn my own boat to the waterline, I can, as long as I don't let the fire spread."

"Hard to do, tied in a slip surrounded by wooden walkways."

"It won't happen. The lumens are lower with this kind of light. Less risk of it being seen through possible cracks in the shades."

I didn't have the gumption to argue. Cal certainly seemed to know what he was doing. He plugged in an electric tea kettle and rummaged in a cupboard while I hastily and surreptitiously tried to get my bearings in the cramped cabin.

I was sitting on a padded bench that I suspected was capable of folding out to meet the bench on the opposite side for a bed. The curved walls were lined with railed shelves, and Cal's sparse belongings were neatly tucked into them. Books—lots and lots of tattered paperbacks, the spines so cracked and worn that I couldn't make out many of the titles. Several dozen hardbacks that were in similar condition, the lettering worn off the covers. A marine radio occupied one nook.

In the galley area where Cal hunched over the minuscule sink, there was one each of the basic implements either hanging from hooks or propped on slotted shelves—tin plate and cup, fork, spoon, butter knife, steak knife, butcher knife, cutting board, bowl, can opener, sauce pan, cast iron frying pan, spatula, tongs. There was also a heavy-duty, battery-operated flashlight— so he did own more modern equipment.

Somehow, observing Cal in his habitat reminded me of the pictures I used to see in children's books about hobos. The ones where the raggedy man with holes in his coat and a scruffy beard held a stick propped on his shoulder with a large handkerchief tied in a bundle around all his worldly possession at the other end.

Cal's sailboat was his bundle, his whole life. Neat and tidy—which was a necessity in a space so small—but very, very meager. I suddenly realized I had nothing to complain about, even with my currently limited income. I probably threw away more stuff than Cal used in a year.

He sidled into the narrow slot between the benches and handed me a steaming mug before taking a seat across from me. His own cup appeared to be the cap from an ancient thermos. One of each essential; no more.

"I should have asked you for help." I sipped the potent brew—some kind of herbal mint concoction that immediately opened my sinuses. "Thank you."

Cal tipped his head, an acknowledging gesture. "You didn't have to ask."

"Were you watching the whole time?"

"Just about. I pulled your kayak up onto the bank just north of the marina. It'll be safe there until tomorrow."

"Operation disintegration," I muttered and took another big gulp. Whatever the drink was, it was going down easy. Warmth radiated out from my core, spreading along my limbs. It was just beginning to prickle at my knees and elbows.

"You need to work on your tradecraft," Cal agreed. "But you got the recorder in place?"

I nodded in wonder. He knew about that too?

"I'm afraid you're going to need that recording in order to convince Vaughn that Norman is a more serious problem than the others have been. I'll swipe it off her deck tomorrow when she's out."

"Wait," I blurted. "You've been keeping an eye on Bettina through *all* of her boyfriends?"

Cal shrugged and slurped.

He wasn't going to answer. I could tell by the way his blue eyes found something to examine on the shelf behind my head. So I brought up another issue that had been bothering me. "I thought you said that style of kayak is the most stable."

My words brought Cal's attention back, along with a quirked smile. "But not foolproof."

Sensitive subject. So I switched topics. A human pinball—that's me. "Why is your boat named *Ecclesiastes*?"

Cal was unperturbed. "Have you read it?"

"The book, you mean? In the Bible?"

He nodded.

"Yeah, parts, I guess. Quite quotable."

Cal took my empty mug and stood. He leaned over the galley counter and poured more of the tea through a strainer, and puffs of fragrant steam rose toward the ceiling. "Read the whole thing. Then we'll talk."

We finished our refills without additional conversation, listening instead to the creak of the *Ecclesiastes* against her lines, the dull thuds of her bumpers hitting the dock finger, the sputtering hiss of the oil lamp's flame, and the wary hoot of an owl in the wildlife refuge.

~oOo~

Things seem smaller and more manageable in daylight. The next morning while I was out on the roof deck luxuriating in the Five Tibetans, another tug rumbled past, nosing a single barge full of sawdust upriver. The resulting wake barely registered as a blip, adding a little sideways loll to my table top stretch position. I did not tumble over.

I doubted three additional barges, as had been the case the prior evening, would make that much difference. In other words, my nighttime expedition had been profoundly ill-conceived, and I needed to get my act together. I also needed to quit putting myself in a position where other people had to rescue me.

I planned to spend the rest of the day pretending that I was a good neighbor, that I hadn't mucked up an espionage attempt, that I hadn't capsized in the nominal wake of a tug with barges, that I was a responsible adult with ordinary concerns. I was suffering no ill health effects from the dunking I'd undergone, and I chalked that up to Cal's homeopathic potion.

Willow bounded into my good intentions while I was still munching my breakfast granola. "Take me shopping," she said when I answered the door. "You'll love it."

As a rule, I don't love shopping. Particularly when my pocketbook is on the empty side. But she was so eager, and she had a large messenger bag slung across her torso, packed to the brim, apparently, judging by all the lumps and bumps under the thick canvas. It seemed my positive answer was a foregone conclusion.

"Okay," I said. "But we have to come up with something extra special to cook for Cal. I owe him big-time."

"Caviar?" Willow chimed. It was probably the fanciest food she'd ever heard of.

"Have you ever eaten caviar?" I asked.

She shook her head, wide-eyed.

"It's gross. Salt-cured fish eggs. Besides, you don't prepare caviar, really. You just eat it off tiny mother-of-pearl spoons. There's nothing you can do to make it taste any better. And the mama sturgeon is killed so her eggs can be harvested."

Willow's expression was rapidly changing from starstruck to repulsed, so I pressed my advantage and continued, "Although some scientists are working on a procedure in which the mama fish is given a treatment that basically induces labor but spares her life. Purists say that type of caviar is inferior though—too mushy."

Willow's face was almost as blue as her hair, and she was making gagging noises.

I nodded with satisfaction. One minor good deed accomplished.

She sat in the passenger seat of my old Volvo and fiddled with the seat levers while also giving me belated instructions about where to turn. We ended up circling several blocks several times, but our first stop was a farmers' market on the Portland State University campus in the South Park Blocks.

I was in heaven, and Willow knew it. She skipped with giddy delight, her blue locks flying, as she led me along the sidewalk past tables mounded high with apples, pears, lettuces, kale, beans, tomatoes in every possible shade from pale yellow to purplish-black, pungent herbs, soft stone fruits, lavender, honey from local bees, wines, specialty cured meats, giant bouquets of gaily-colored flowers. My head was swimming.

"Kid, you are so not helping with the cash flow," I moaned.

"I don't see any caviar," she answered perkily, "so you're saving money by not buying that." For such a smart-aleck remark, I made her carry my already loaded shopping bag so that I could fill the other one too.

"What are we cooking for Cal?" she asked.

"I have no idea. But whatever it is, with how fresh these ingredients are"—I held the cut stem end of a Tuscan cantaloupe under my nose and inhaled deeply—"it can't help but be marvelous."

I'm not sure if I dragged Willow away, or if she dragged me away, but we finally staggered to the car with bulging bags hanging from our arms. I was ready for a nap, but Willow insisted that the next stop would be just as good.

"Maybe even better." She cast a sly glance at me out of the corner of her eye and giggled.

And so she directed me to Powell's City of Books, a ramshackle city block of old warehouse-style buildings and rooms jammed up against each other with ramps and staircases leading every which way. They had to color-code the rooms so people wouldn't get lost. But I got lost anyway, in the Orange Room, amid the towering stacks of cookbooks for the better part of an hour while Willow browsed the sci-fi section in the Gold Room. I managed to restrain my purchases to just two books—tree and bird identification field guides which Willow helped me pick out.

"Mercy," I breathed once we were safely in the car again.

"Nope. One more," Willow insisted. "Besides, aren't you hungry?"

Which was true. I was starving. Shopping must increase my metabolic rate.

Willow's final destination was only a short distance away, under the Burnside Bridge—the Portland Saturday Market, with rows and rows of small booths featuring local artists and handmade goods. Hats, paintings, photographs, clothing and textiles, metalworking, jewelry, carved wooden toys, soaps, pottery, and wood prints galore. I stumbled at Willow's heels, gawking at all the trinkets and bright colors which were interspersed with the occasional truly spectacular item that caught my eye. A blue-speckled ceramic pitcher, for example, or a long woolen scarf in a striking plaid.

"Come on." Willow tugged on my arm, and we eventually made it through the throngs to the row of food booths closest to the river. I chose Cape Cod-style fish and chips, while Willow devoured a churro and slurped a mango smoothie.

"We're going to have to talk about your nutritional choices," I said with my mouth full.

She shrugged. "It's Saturday."

I was about to point out that stomachs don't know what day of the week it is, but she jumped to her feet and tossed the paper wrappings from our lunch in the trash.

"There's somebody you need to see on the way out."

It struck me, as I trailed her through the crowd, that her blue hair was particularly helpful in situations like this. It provided an easy beacon to spot and follow.

Willow skidded to a stop at a booth on the corner of one of the many pathway intersections. *Bits & Baubs* read the plaque hanging from the awning. And inside was a familiar orange-haired lady who was clanking and jangling her way through a sale of earrings to a middle-aged woman and her daughter. I gaped when I saw how much money exchanged hands. I hated to think how much the bangles Bettina had given me were worth.

Bettina's face split into a joyous smile when she saw us, flooding me in a poignant swamp of guilt, embarrassment, and chagrin over my behavior the night before. I had to quickly arrange my features in what I hoped was a look of delighted surprise.

"Are you having a girls' day out?" Bettina crowed. "How marvelous. Willow, sweetheart, have you seen the new abalone dangles I've made?"

But Bettina was interrupted by yet another customer with money clenched in her fist, and commerce ensued while Willow and I waited.

"How was your dinner last night?" I blurted when Bettina returned to us. I deliberately chose the word *dinner* instead of *date*, hoping she would note my interest in the food rather than the man and so that she would have a chance to slink an answer past Willow without admitting to any romantic intentions.

But my subtleties went unheeded.

"Oh, Norman. Well—" Bettina fanned her hands in front of her face.

I couldn't tell if the gesture meant that Norman made Bettina's temperature rise—as though he was a source of rampant sexual appeal—or if she was waving him off as a nonstarter. And then a young man on the other side of the booth had some questions about a carved wood bracelet he was thinking of buying for his girlfriend, and we lost Bettina to the demands of her business once again.

Willow was far too keen to have missed the undercurrent, so I whispered to her, "What do you think that means? Are we going to have Norman hanging around the marina, being a pest?"

She snorted. "I'd bet a month's worth of lunch money on it." Then she groaned. "Another one. We haven't recovered from Nigel yet. When old guys get the hots, they can be *soooo* annoying." The statement was accompanied by a dramatic eye roll, and it was my turn to snort.

"Oh, girls, I'm so sorry." Bettina rushed back. "Watch, in twenty minutes, there'll be a complete dearth of customers, but right now..." Her brown eyes darted toward a woman who was holding a pair of flashy silver hoops up next to her ears while peering into one of the many mirrors Bettina had installed around the booth.

"It's all right," I said quickly. "We'll catch up later."

Bettina fluttered her fingers at us and turned to help the woman decide just how extravagantly large a pair of earrings she could wear without bonking herself in the nose with them when she shook her head. It was a criterion I had never considered before.

Willow was quiet in the car on the way home. Too quiet.

Moodiness? Fatigue? An introvert who'd used up all her social reserves?

I didn't want to pry—my track record at helpful prying being somewhat dismal at the moment—but I also wanted Willow to feel comfortable talking with me. So I opted for a non-threatening observation. "I noticed that Bettina's house is called *Dock's End*, and the one next to it, where Boris and Petula live, is called *River Haven*. Is that common, for people to name their floating houses? I mean, I get it that boats have names, but floating houses too?"

"Oh yeah," Willow said eagerly. "You should name yours. *Tin Can* might be nice, now that the cargo containers are painted gray."

I don't know why it struck me as so funny. Tin Can. But it was. I laughed until I had to wipe tears from the corners of my eyes. I think it was the idea—when the time came—of admitting to my father that I lived in a tin can that sent me into hysterics.

"Done," I finally wheezed. "I'll find a jazzy font and something to paint it on."

Willow beamed.

CHAPTER 15

I had to admit Willow had been an excellent tour guide. I wanted to repay her kindness, so I invited her on a combo business/pleasure outing that evening—to the soft opening of the Wicked Bean Annex, and in so doing, I thrilled her little heart to the core.

"Darren's too old for you," I warned. "And you can't have any alcohol tonight. Strictly coffee."

"I know, I know," she muttered, but her pale gray eyes sparkled.

I didn't want to come across as too dictatorial, but I did also mention that since it was a special occasion, conservative, arty, and bohemian—but with a classy flair—attire would be appropriate. I tried not to chuckle as I said it, and was anxiously awaiting what ensemble Willow would come up with. As long as it was an improvement over her hoodie, ratty jeans, and scuffed sneakers, I'd be happy.

Frankly, I felt a pair of Bettina's dangly earrings was in order, so I trotted over to her house along the floating walkway maze and left a note taped to her front door. I also took the opportunity to lean around the corner of her river-facing deck and verify that my audio recorder was no longer where I'd left it.

Which led me back to Cal's slip and the *Ecclesiastes* tugging at her lines. But Cal wasn't home either, or at least he didn't respond when I knelt and pounded on the hull with my fist.

He had returned my kayak, however, including the paddle. How he'd retrieved them both, I couldn't fathom, but there they were—the kayak upside-down and lashed on my rear deck with the paddle tucked underneath, the way I always stored them.

I spent the next hour examining my wardrobe. As I had been made acutely aware of over the past several days, Portland was nothing like Washington D.C. in terms of fashion. All my tailored skirt and jacket ensembles, the pantyhose, the moderately-heeled pumps, and the pressed white blouses constituted overkill of the most snobbish variety. The only way they'd be useful to me now was if I separated them and used them individually. And the pantyhose not at all. I threw every single pair in the trash. I can't even begin to describe how wonderful that felt.

I was in the middle of pulling my clothes from their hangers in the closet and heaping them into piles on the floor by season when a knock sounded on the front door. I rushed into the living room and flung open the door, expecting Bettina and a fountain of unsolicited advice which I felt in a particularly good mood to endure. But instead Cal stood there, furtively glancing over his shoulder. He pushed his way inside and latched the door behind him.

"Here," he nudged a small black box into my hand—my recorder.

"Have you listened to it?" I whispered, wondering as I did so why such secrecy inside my own house was necessary. Cal's mannerisms were rubbing off on me.

"The guy's a crook."

"I thought so," I growled. "Twenty percent. Nothing in the stock market guarantees any return, let alone twenty percent."

"It gets worse." Cal nodded toward the recorder. "Vaughn needs to know."

I started a little, took a step backward. "Uh, that's a problem. You see, Bettina trusted me with this, and if I go blabbing..." I narrowed my eyes at Cal. "Wait. Why *are* you so watchful? Are you on Vaughn's payroll or something?" I wasn't quite ready to buy the excuse that old habits die hard, although that was probably true too.

"Bettina's the closest thing I've got to a mother," Cal mumbled. "Her parties aren't my cup of tea, but I like to look out for her."

"Okay. So that's you, me, and I'm pretty sure Willow has a good grasp on the situation as well." I sighed. "We ought to be able to handle it, just the three of us."

The door behind me rattled with an insistent knock. I flinched but managed to check the peephole this time.

"Bettina," I hissed, and tossed the recorder to Cal. I pointed deeper into the house. "Turn the lights off."

He was gone—silently, speedily, and for the second time in less than a week, I had a man hiding in my bedroom.

I opened the front door.

Bettina came bearing three shallow, stackable trays. "Darling, if you'd told me at the booth today, I would have sent you home with my newest creation, a pair of amethyst and silver bicone bead delights. They look like chandeliers on the ears."

"I was hoping for something subtle and demure," I muttered.

"Nonsense. Do you know how much inventory I have? Absolutely a delight to give these a public showing." Bettina plunked the trays on the kitchen counter and spread them out.

"How much do you have invested in your business?" I asked, cringing at the impertinence of my own question.

Bettina shrugged, sending her cascade of necklaces jingling. "It's all I have to do, in my dotage. Either that or the money sits in the bank. And I enjoy it, the creative process, figuring out new combinations and techniques."

All that money, huh? No wonder Norman found her tantalizing. I gritted my teeth and bent to admire the selection of earrings on display.

"What are you wearing tonight?" Bettina asked. And before I could stop her, she was marching toward my bedroom, moving very fast for such a tiny lady. I skittered in her wake.

But when she flicked on the lights, there were just piles of clothes scattered on the floor. I quickly glanced into the open closet—hangers, a laundry basket, but no man—and exhaled.

Talk about tradecraft. Cal was a disappearing genius. He must have gone out through the French doors, but the lever on the handle was still in the locked position. I shook my head in wonder.

Bettina, however, was nudging through my piles with the tip of her faux-croc, pointy-toed, kitten-heeled shoe, her hands firmly planted on her hips. If she noticed or cared that there was no bed in the bedroom, she didn't say so. But the dismal condition of my wardrobe appeared to be causing her palpable distress.

"The only good thing you have is that little yellow number you wore to my party," she sniffed.

"I need something warmer for tonight, and more professional."

"Professional?" Bettina arched her left brow at me. "Darling, you should try sexy sometime." She held up a be-ringed index finger before I could object. "I get it, I get it—not tonight."

Except the outfit she finally coerced me into was on the sexy side. Sexy professional. I tried to convince myself I was starting a new trend while I examined my reflection in the full-length mirror and tugged on my hemline.

Willow opened the front door and yoo-hooed in lieu of knocking. She appeared in the bedroom doorway bedecked in a corseted steampunk thing—all pink satin and black ribbons with a poufy tulle skirt and black leather motorcycle boots. She flung a short hooded cape over her shoulders and twirled for us. She looked like a pink (with blue hair) version of Little Red Riding Hood on her way home from a night of playing strip poker at a biker bar. At least she'd won more than she'd lost. I wondered if Roxy had seen her before she'd left the apartment.

"Perfect!" Bettina clasped her hands over her heart and smiled beatifically at her. My role model—oh joy. Also, I should be careful what I wish for—or at the very least, what I suggest to others.

It was with an odd mix of gratitude and guilt that I bade farewell to Bettina and set off with Willow in my faithful old Volvo. These two women, at opposite ends of the age spectrum, were my first real friends in my new town. I hated the idea that I might be on the verge of betraying one of them and co-opting the other one into helping me do so.

~oOo~

If the crowd at Wicked Bean and the Annex next door was any indicator, Darren had a smashing success on his hands.

Willow and I waded through the packed bodies to the coffee counter and ordered drinks. After that, I lost immediate, arm's-reach contact with her, although she was very easy to spot in the melee.

It's one of the nice things about being tall—still having a good view even if the venue is congested. Another perk is the opportunity to catch snatches of conversation that rise above the general hubbub and to have a chance to link the words with the speakers since I can see them.

If I'd had my audio recorder with me, I would have been able to score at least a dozen raving reviews. But at this point, I didn't think Darren needed much more marketing or publicity efforts from me. It was all going swimmingly, and I hated to think what the fire marshal might say about the official grand opening scheduled for the following weekend based on the size of the horde of happy, caffeinated, chattering people attending this preliminary event.

Not surprisingly, some of the conversations were about Ian Thorpe and the investigation into his murder. They were speculative and repetitive, and while I tried to tune them out, a few registered in my consciousness. I heard a lot more women's names associated with Ian's—continuing confirmation of his tomcatting ways. And for all the awareness his activism had brought to environmental issues, it seemed he might be remembered most—at least locally—for his promiscuity. A sad epitaph indeed.

So when I heard the words *sensor* and *readings*, my ears perked up. Nothing like a scientific conversation to pique a girl's interest.

Except it wasn't scientific. It couldn't be—because the speaker was a bedraggled young man in black. I don't mean to stereotype, but the boy was barely old enough to shave, and scientists generally have a series of letters after their names that requires several years of torture at an institute of higher learning, which also tends to alter their appearance somewhat. Not that the young man was making much effort to sculpt his facial hair. The soul patch under his lower lip boasted five individual black hairs—more like a straggle than an actual patch.

I also didn't think he was trying to make a fashion statement with his monochromatic clothing—it seemed more likely that he didn't own any other colors. Easy to get dressed in the morning when everything matches. His outfit reminded me of how much clearer things were in high school where everyone delineated their affiliations by their appearance, and complex nuances of personality were either explicitly suppressed or so very blaring as to be completely muddled.

He was crouched low over a table near the wall with two similarly dressed buddies. They all had the pallor and rapidly-blinking eyes of the chronically housebound. Even at a special occasion like this, their default setting was to hunker and lurk at the edges.

He was still talking, and I caught a few more snippets. "Threshold...alarm...override and send false feedback within certain parameters."

Which was mightily intriguing. I waved to Willow across the room, and eventually she realized that I was signaling to her. We pushed through the throng toward each other and met in the middle.

"Do you know that boy?" I hollered near her ear, trying to surreptitiously point at the young man in question.

She snorted. "Those geeks? Yeah, they go to my school."

"They live in Fidelity?" I squeaked.

"I can't help it if we're not all geniuses and supermodels," Willow grumbled.

"I need you to introduce me to the one with the soul patch."

This request earned me a look of absolute incredulity. "If I recall correctly, you're the one who so condescendingly pointed out that Darren is too *old* for me. *You* could be Cy's *mother*. And that's just gross."

"Not that kind of introduction," I hissed, steaming at her sudden sense of Victorian propriety. "I need to ask him technical questions, and I need street cred with him; otherwise he'll just blow me off as some nosy old lady."

"Uh-huh."

But I could tell the idea pleased her. I suppose there's a certain amount of cachet in being able to introduce an older, mysterious woman to one of your peers.

Willow clomped through the crowd and pulled up abruptly at the boys' table. All three heads popped up, and their eyes took on a desperate quality as though they were searching for crevices to flee into.

She stabbed a finger at the young man with the soul patch. "Cyrus Watson." Then she turned and stabbed the same finger at me. "Eva Fairchild. She's my neighbor, and for some crazy reason, she wants to talk to you." With a flip of her blue hair, Willow stalked off.

"Hello, Cy," I said in my smoothest voice. I grabbed a recently vacated chair and spun it around before the previous occupant could reclaim it. I scooted up to the boys' table and hunched in with them.

"Are you into programming?" I asked.

"Uh, yeah," he stammered.

The other boys snickered.

"Do you do custom jobs—you know, a little on the side?" I asked.

Cy's flush deepened and his neck disappeared into his shoulders. "It's just a hobby."

"But I bet you're really good. Not too many people can do that sort of thing—case out a system, figure out how it works, alter the results, and redirect copies of the reports."

"Yeah," he said warily, his eyes narrowing.

I pulled a twenty-dollar bill out of my purse and pushed it across the table toward the other boys. "How about if you two hunks get yourselves more to drink?" I said with a wink.

They almost knocked over their chairs while scrabbling to their feet. They left the table quickly but not without some rather bawdy gaping and punching Cy's shoulders in a congratulatory manner.

"I overheard enough to know," I said once I had Cy's full attention again, "that you've been hacking."

"But—" he spluttered. He gripped the edge of the table with white-knuckled fingers, and I was afraid he was going to bolt.

"It's okay," I said quickly. "I realize it's just a matter of curiosity and testing your skills. A way of learning and improving, matching your wits against the original designers'."

Cy snorted softly, but he stayed seated. "So?" he muttered with a surly grimace.

"So—you're most recent project—the one with the thresholds and alarm overrides?" I kept my voice low and tried desperately *not* to sound like a teacher or a mother or any other disapproving authority figure. "Did it also involve mercury readings? *Hg* on the periodic table?" I added in case chemistry wasn't his strong suit.

Cy's eyes suddenly found lots of other places to look besides at me. "How do you know?" he whispered.

"I've seen one of the batches of results."

His eyes grew even rounder, and tendons lifted in his neck. He actually levitated off the chair an inch before I was able to lay a reassuring hand on his arm.

"Not from you. As far as I know, your bypass is secure. These results were older."

Cy seemed to crumple and buried his face in his hands. "I am so in trouble." The words came out muffled and distorted, and I was afraid he was going to start crying. "It seemed like fun. I found the job on one of those anonymous hacker boards. What the original poster was asking for was so easy I couldn't believe no one else had signed up for the job yet. The data from those off-the-shelf systems is unencrypted; anybody can see it and play with it. It sounded like a practical joke, like he was messing with his friend's experiment or something. No harm, no foul?" Cy peeked over his fingers hopefully, as though I might be able to absolve him of his sins, or at least of the consequences.

"Did he follow through and pay you?" I asked.

Cy shrugged. "Ten bitcoins. I cashed them out right away. Those things are unstable and get seized all the time. A little risky for a seventeen-year-old." His voice was tinged with wry humor. "At least a seventeen-year-old with my set of parents."

I straightened and let him see my amazement. I didn't even have to ham it up. "Wow."

"No kidding." Cy leaned forward, eager now. "There's no rule against taking advantage of a sucker, right? The job was so stupid easy, and it bought me a new desktop with an incredible graphics card and—"

I held up a hand to stop him since I knew he would vault into language I didn't understand regarding processor speed and terabytes. "So you thought your client was playing a prank?"

Cy shrugged again. "Or something."

"I think it might be more serious than that. Thirty-five hundred bucks? Some joke."

If Cy was surprised that I knew the approximate current value of bitcoins, he didn't show it. But from the way he slumped in his seat and fiddled with the handle of his mug, I figured he'd also followed this thought trail in his own mind, and it had left his conscience appropriately uncomfortable in spite of the generous remuneration—or quite possibly because of it.

"Look, I can't make you do it, but I think you need to talk to Detective Malloy of the Fidelity Police Department." I fished in my purse for the card Vaughn had given me and slid it across the table to Cy. "He's pretty cool, and he won't jump to conclusions. But he is investigating a murder. I think the owner of the system you hacked was Ian Thorpe."

The name had an immediate impact on Cy. He blanched and blinked and snatched his hand back from Vaughn's card as though it was covered in slug slime. "No way," he whispered.

I nodded. "Which means your client may have had an ulterior motive."

"No way," Cy whispered again, but he stretched his hand back out and picked up the card with trembling fingers. "I won't be able to go on that forum ever again. My cover will be blown. So much for anonymity."

"Not necessarily. You can trust Detective Malloy's discretion."

Willow plopped down in the chair across the table from me. "Anything juicy?" she said loudly, making direct eye contact with me, which served the obvious purpose of treating Cy as though he didn't exist.

I grinned at her. The lovely awkwardness of teenagerdom. I'd be willing to bet she had a crush on Cy too. Or probably on any boy who had the potential of displaying kindness toward her, even if his true feelings were masked with churlishness. So much posturing.

But her interruption was fortuitous.

Cy needed time to think over his responsibilities, and my continued presence would not be helpful. I could always tip off Vaughn about the possible connection, but it would be so much better all around if Cy would make the decision to come forward himself. I figured I'd give him twenty-four hours. The user records on the anonymous hacker forum were probably safe for the time being, as long as no one alerted the forum administrator.

So far the only people who would have reason to do that were me, Cy, and Cy's client. And if the client hadn't tried to cover his digital tracks yet, he probably wasn't going to. The average, gullible citizen tends to trust the designation *anonymous* even when there's no legitimate reason to do so.

I pushed to standing. "Juicy, no. Sleepy, yes. I'm so *old* that I need to call it a night and get home to bed."

"Geez. Last time I'm coming to a party with you." Willow flounced out of her chair and produced an exaggerated hip wiggle as she brushed by Cy.

The voluminous tulle skirt had a nullifying effect on her efforts, however, so I wasn't too worried. Cy had other things on his mind.

CHAPTER 16

In spite of the excuse I'd given Willow, my excitement for the remainder of the evening was searching my bedroom. I had a feeling Cal had stashed the audio recorder somewhere in my piles of clothes.

And I was right. He'd found a safe spot underneath a pair of fuzzy flannel pajama bottoms that had little dancing robots printed on them—a Christmas gift from my dad's fifth wife.

Norman's tinny recorded words shot me straight to foaming outrage. "Ooooo!" I spluttered and punched the replay button for a second dose of indignation.

Cal's categorization of Norman as a crook was a serious understatement. The guy was running a Ponzi scheme, pure and simple. And from the desperate promises he'd made to Bettina, it was obvious he was under pressure from his earlier investors. He needed new money and fast. There was nothing subtle about his overtures for funds. The problem was he was smooth—smooth enough that from Bettina's answers she appeared to believe his professed infatuation. At the very least, she hadn't discouraged him—either romantically or financially.

Although she had shown a bit of spine in insisting that their next date be on his dime. Not in so many words, but she'd sounded the slightest bit miffed when he'd suggested that she invite him over for another meal. He'd also gone overboard with excessive flattery of her cooking.

What a moocher. Made me wonder just how hard up Norman was. Could he even afford a Quarter Pounder with Cheese?

And made me realize there was only one way I could do the right thing on all fronts. I would have to come clean.

~oOo~

Bright and early the next morning, after tossing ineffectually on the mattress for a couple of hours and no sleep, I pounded on the private apartment entrance at the side of the marina office. Roxy answered the door, already coiffed and with a cigarette stub coiling its last vestiges of smoke from between her fingers.

"I'm in trouble," I said.

"How much?" Roxy said, absolutely unfazed.

I blinked. "It's hard to quantify, actually."

She blew out an exasperated breath. "Inches or feet?"

"What?" I squinted at her.

She returned the squint. "Water. Isn't that why you're here? Is your house taking on water? How much determines who we call." She checked the watch on her wrist, dropping ash as she did so, and shook her head. "At the crack of dawn on a Sunday morning is going to cost you *beaucoup* bucks, no matter how deep it is."

Nothing like the possibility of a flood worthy of the word-a-day calendar to put my problems into perspective.

"It's not that," I said hurriedly. "Relational issues. I sort of need Willow—for moral support."

Roxy barked a laugh and wheezed until her eyes watered. "Is that so?" Then she returned to squinting. "You're serious, aren't you?"

When I nodded, she opened the door to its full width and beckoned me inside with the cigarette hand. "Good luck then. Her bedroom's at the end of the hall. Sleeps like the dead." Her face tightened, and she quickly amended, "Like the comatose, actually. Vital signs intact, but no response. Maybe you'll get better results than I usually do."

I tried an old trick I learned at summer camp from my first truly tomboy friend—the amazing and fearless Jeannie Corallo of Queens, New York. I blew hard into Willow's ear and immediately bent backward out of the way of whatever might come up swinging.

She bolted upright, hair and eyes wild, thrashing at the covers. "What the—"

"Good morning," I said. "I need help."

"Aaargh." Willow flopped back on the bed and pressed a pillow over her face.

"Want to watch some abject humility in action?" I asked.

One gray eye peeked around the embroidered rose on the pillowcase.

I quickly outlined what I'd learned the previous night and stressed the importance of an expeditious confession.

Willow pushed herself up and sat cross-legged facing me. "What a creep," she hissed.

"Exactly. Preys on older, lonely women, I suspect, although I don't want to word it that way to Bettina. With two of us there, she can't flip out too badly, can she?"

Willow shook her head, sending the tangle of blue hair flying. "I don't think Bettina ever flips out. She's actually pretty cool. But yeah, you need backup. Just give me a minute." She climbed out of bed and began rummaging through the closet.

I waited for her outside, with my arms wrapped around my torso in an attempt to quell the shivering. Even though the days had been sunny, the nights—and early mornings—were getting downright chilly. My breath formed steam droplets that drifted downwind in sparse clouds.

Willow and I would have to go it alone. Cal hadn't answered my knock, so I hadn't been able to ask his opinion. Without his permission, I couldn't reveal how my ineptitude with a kayak had forced his participation in the matter. But maybe Bettina would respond better if she thought it was a girls-only predicament anyway.

Willow emerged dressed for combat. No flirty overtones today. Straight up motorcycle boots, ripped jeans, and an olive-drab canvas jacket that looked as if it had come off the clearance rack at the army surplus store. I wholeheartedly agreed.

We clumped down the gangplank and tromped along the floating walkways—all the way to the very north end. If Bettina hadn't been awake before, she was now. I pounded loudly on her front door.

She answered wearing a gigantic gaudy Hawaiian-print shirt backwards on her scrawny frame and a pair of half-glasses with the thickest prescription I had ever seen. The top shirt button was fastened at the back of her neck, and the crazy coverall hung in loose palm-frond-and-parrot folds over her front.

"Got the groove on?" Willow asked while simultaneously shoving in front of me and barging inside.

Bettina chuckled and backed out of the way, motioning to me to follow. "Yes, dear. It doesn't cure the insomnia, but it slightly redeems the time." She turned on her heel and led us down the hallway to the spare bedroom.

Which turned out to be her incredibly organized and glittering jewelry studio. One glance around, and I suspected Willow had had a hand in the setup, which perhaps explained why she was so comfortable making herself at home on the tufted club chair in the corner. She kicked her boots off and tucked her feet up underneath herself with a pointed look at me.

Bettina had settled behind a sturdy desk that was strewn with pretty peach-colored glass beads in a shallow working tray. A necklace appeared to be undergoing assembly. "You're out early," she said brightly, tilting her chin and pursing her lips so that she could peer through the lenses of her glasses at the fine filament end of the necklace string.

"I have a dreadful, awful, no-good secret to tell you," I announced.

Bettina's brown eyes flew above the half-moons of her glasses and focused on me like laser beams. "Is this about Norman?"

The breath caught in my throat, but I pushed past it. "Yes," I said firmly. Then I pressed on even faster, wanting to get out the short version before her defensive hackles got any higher. "I did something I'm not proud of, but in so doing I've also learned that he's a conman."

Bettina very carefully and precisely set the necklace down on the felt-lined tray and took an additional moment to slide a few stray beads into place with her fingertips. "Drat," she finally said. "But I'm not surprised." She flashed a thoughtful glance at Willow. "I suppose this calls for hot cocoa."

Willow's face split into a charmingly sweet smile, so tender and unassuming that I was momentarily stunned by its glory. She scooted off the chair and whispered, "I told you," as she brushed past me.

"You have quite a lot of explaining to do, young lady," Bettina said sternly, but she sidled out from behind the desk, took my arm, and guided me to the kitchen.

I dumped the story—sans Cal's role—before my marshmallows had melted. Then I briefly outlined how a Ponzi scheme works. It just felt so good to let it all out, and Bettina was bearing it remarkably well, if quietly.

"I thought I heard a splash," she murmured. "Good heavens, you must have been chilled to the bone."

I pulled the audio recorder out of my pocket and laid it on the counter, but Bettina impatiently waved a manicured hand. "I *know* what I said. And I remember very clearly what Norman said. Pushy bastard."

Attagirl. Nothing heals a broken heart like a healthy dose of righteous indignation. Willow and I shared tentative but hopeful grins from behind our mugs.

Bettina scowled and traced the fleur-de-lis design on her mug with a fingernail. "If he doesn't get the money from me, then he'll go after someone else, won't he? Someone like me—a widow with a trusting heart and too much time on her hands. Maybe even someone desperate who couldn't afford that kind of loss." Her brows pitched up into peaks, and she studied my face. "I'm not sure *I* could survive that kind of loss. My investments—well, you know retirement isn't what it used to be. I have to be careful."

I nodded. "We all do."

"Bastard," she muttered again, with more venom this time. "What made you suspect?"

"When you told me he wanted to review your financial situation." I shrugged. "That's about the same as a dentist insisting on examining your fillings on a first date. Reeks of ulterior motives."

Bettina's palm smacked down hard on the counter. "He's not going to get away with it. Not if I can help it." She turned and rustled through a stack of miscellaneous papers—the kind that accumulate in the hub of a house— and produced a small black address book. In a flash, she was dialing her phone with her other hand, her thumb punching the buttons with a speed that rivaled any teenage gamer's.

"Karleen," she said into the receiver. "Bettina here. I have a doozy of a fraud case for you. Time sensitive. But the info comes as a straight trade. You have to let me in on the fun if you want to pursue it. And you will. Call me." She hung up.

"Detective Jett?" Willow asked, her voice hushed as though she was in awe.

"You betcha." Bettina's orange bob swished vigorously with her nodding. "Can't tell Vaughn. And Karleen will slap cuffs on old Norman before he has time to think crossways. She doesn't take guff from anybody."

"A female detective? With the Fidelity Police Department?" I asked, hoping for some clarity in the rapidly changing emotional landscape.

Willow just grinned at me, but Bettina answered. "Yep. Karleen Jett. First—and so far, only—to break the detective gender barrier in the department. She and Arthur went through the academy together; we go way back, since the late '60s. She works non-violent cases now, as a sort of concession before being put entirely out to pasture. Her knees aren't what they used to be—can't hoof it after punks anymore. I happen to know Vaughn thinks the world of her, and she keeps that chief of his in line, that's for sure." Bettina nodded. "I'll be in good hands."

"Wait a minute," I said slowly. "What are you planning?"

"A sting, of course. Tuesday night. During my next date with Norman. I'll wear a wire, catch him in the act." Bettina had shoved the magnifying glasses to the top of her head and stood with her tiny fists planted on her narrow hips beneath the billowing makeshift smock. The palm fronds were aquiver with her unbridled rancor.

I thought she'd watched too much true-crime television. There was no way Vaughn would let his mother get into a sticky scenario like that—if he knew.

I hadn't met Detective Jett at or after the press conference, and I couldn't announce that I'd met Chief Monk without being probed about the details surrounding that event. I clamped my mouth shut. Bettina was a grown woman, and she was showing considerable pluck. Who was I to stifle her initiative, especially since it had only reached the bravado stage at the moment?

I still couldn't help myself. Horrible scenes of Norman hollering, red-faced, and wine glasses smashed on the floor flooded my mind. What if he went further, assaulted Bettina physically? She'd already had enough of that for one lifetime. "What if he figures it out?" I blurted. "Who will protect you? He's tall, and much bigger than you are, and if he gets angry..."

"You're not the only one who can go undercover." Bettina's eyes narrowed into an expression that would brook no further argument. "I'll pull it off. You just watch."

I sighed and returned to chewing my lip. It would be up to the prudence and discretion of Detective Jett to dissuade Bettina at this point. At least I could be sure Bettina wasn't going to go all gooey over Norman and risk her nest egg.

My duty was completed, but, boy, had I ever opened up a whole new can of worms.

CHAPTER 17

There is no peace for the busybody. My phone rang as Willow and I were retracing our steps along the floating walkways.

"Did you give my card to a seventeen-year-old kid named Cyrus Watson at a party last night?" Vaughn said.

"I did."

There were several seconds of contemplative breathing on the other end of the line, then Vaughn said, "Thanks."

"You're welcome." Only to find that Vaughn hadn't hung around for the usual social niceties as my answer hit the dead white noise of a disconnected call. But his cursory manner couldn't dampen my exultant chuckle.

"What?" Willow asked, peering up at me.

"Your friend Cy just proved himself to be an honorable man."

She snorted.

"I'm serious." I poked her in the shoulder with a stiff forefinger. "Pay attention. These little details—they matter big time in the real world. Mark my words."

The blue hair shielded her face, but I'm pretty sure she graced my admonishment with an eye-roll. But no matter—unsolicited advice was the price of admission if she wanted to hang out with me. There was plenty more to come.

And then I remembered. I inhaled sharply and halted on the walkway. "I'm so sorry. I'm keeping you from your writing group this morning."

Willow shrugged. "It's the same old same old all the time, anyway."

I was certain she was downplaying her disappointment. Roxy had portrayed this Sunday morning ritual as something Willow insisted upon.

"You mean you'd rather plan a covert sting operation than sip coffee with your fellow wordsmiths?" I asked playfully.

She nodded with a sly peek at me. "Pretty much. Life sure has spiced up around here since you moved in."

"Terrific," I muttered. "But maybe I can make it up to you. How would you like a day of slaving over the stove?"

I was exaggerating, of course, but she took on the challenge with a spritely, "Sure!"

When we got to my house, we ransacked my fridge and pantry. And that activity was a delight in and of itself since I had a wealth of potential ingredients from our trip to the farmers' market.

Finally, we settled on a menu, and while I brewed our first coffee of the day, I dispatched Willow to try knocking on the *Ecclesiastes'* hull again.

"Invitation issued," she announced upon her return. She slid the clean pan that had previously contained lasagna onto the counter. "Although I can report for a fact that Cal's not gaining weight. I caught him doing laundry."

"Not yet," I countered. "Give me a month, and he'll look healthier."

Then we commenced leisurely cooking lessons intermixed with actual preparation, technique tips, sampling, sniffing, and general exploring of the sensual wonders that are fresh foods recently plucked from their native habitat. Willow proved to be a ready convert.

After the chicken pieces had been seared and handfuls of trimmed and chopped veggies had been coated in a thickening roux and doused with white wine in the Dutch oven along with a bouquet garni, Willow set to hand-lettering a menu card for Cal's benefit while I applied artistic touches to my house's new sign.

I finished more quickly than she did because "Tin Can" is much easier to spell than all the French words she kept asking me how to pronounce.

"There," she finally said with satisfaction, sliding the card across for me to see. With typical Willow flair, it was a fait accompli, the lack of correctly-placed accent marks notwithstanding:

Gremolata butter on rustic artisan bread

Light-deprived, milder inner leaves of chicorée frisée (also known as curly endive—we'd had a long discussion about this, along with significant sampling of the leaves in their various shades of green), **radish, and Tuscan cantaloupe salad dressed with lemon-mustard vinaigrette**

White coq au vin à la Eva (because I'd modified the recipe to suit the seasonal vegetables and to make it more summery)

Orange-rind infused local blackberry honey (instead of the traditional hard, thin caramel that usually tops true crème brûlée because how could I resist that amazing honey at the farmers' market?) **drizzled over vanilla custard**

"Perfect," I said. "Lots of citrus, but that's okay."

Willow tore a chunk out of the bread and swiped it through the herbed butter before I could smack her hand away.

"It's better if you wait," I said. "Your own cooking tastes best with company."

Cal arrived a few minutes early and hung up the house's nameplate for me while Willow and I dressed the salad and sliced the bread.

It was a Sunday dinner for the ages. We laughed, told stories, shared anecdotes, and Cal even revealed tidbits of his past. Not enough for me to string together a rough time line, but clues nonetheless, and intimations of possible reasons for some of his oddities.

Watching Willow scoop another serving of coq au vin from the tureen and sop up the juice with a hunk of bread made me realize how much I'd missed during the hectic pace of my Washington D.C. life. No one relaxed there; no one lingered over dessert there; no one revealed their true selves there. I savored the deliciousness of the occasion that went far beyond food.

We were sipping coffee and dipping into a bowl of after-harvest muscat grapes which were so tiny and sweet that they were even better than the raisins they would have become if they'd been left on the vines another week when Vaughn found us on the rear deck. With a wry pitch to his brows and his hands stuffed in his pockets, he took in the scene—Cal and me sprawled in rather ungainly fashion on the two rough and splintery Adirondack chairs the previous owner had left behind instead of hauling to the dump and Willow flat on her stomach on the decking with one hand dangling in the water. Who could blame us? Our bellies were full and we were steeped in a sort of lethargic contentment, soaking in the day's last warm rays of sunshine.

"Welcome to the *Tin Can*," I said with a lazy flourish.

"Uh-huh," Vaughn grunted, either not impressed or not willing to participate in the languid mood.

Cal straightened and nudged Willow with his toe. "Dish duty. You and me, kiddo." After he'd levered himself to his feet, he fished a handful of black wires and crunched plastic shards from the side cargo pocket of his shorts. He shoved the handful toward Vaughn. "This one is damaged. Hit by floating debris, most likely. I found several others intact and left them in place. I'll draw you a diagram of their locations if you want."

By this time, I'd sat up straighter too, my curiosity radar on full alert. But Cal and Willow hurried inside, and I was left with a detective who was displaying his signature potent grouchiness.

He eased into the chair Cal had vacated, stretched out his long legs, and fixed his stare on the river.

As I have noted before, I can out-silence just about anyone—I've found it to be an extremely useful skill. I mirrored Vaughn's posture and let the tense gulf build.

"Thanks again," Vaughn finally said.

I risked a tiny sidelong glance at him but kept my mouth shut.

"For urging Cy to come forward," he continued. "The kid had no absolutely no idea of the value of his information. I've submitted an expedited request to the regional computer forensics lab. They'll be at their desks tomorrow, and they should give my case priority since it's possibly murder-related."

"Does that mean Frank Cox has jumped to the top of your suspect list?" I asked.

Vaughn just grunted again and clinked together the pieces of broken gadget in his hand. "Know what this is?" he asked, opening his palm a little so I could see.

"I'm going to guess it's one of Ian's sensors."

Another grunt. "Cal and his legendary kayaking skills. If anyone could find the sensors now that Ian's gone, I knew it would be him." Vaughn sighed audibly, a long, drawn-out exhale. "Without the lab results, I can't pin the hacking-for-hire on Cox just now, but that doesn't mean I can't bring him in for more questioning. See if he squirms when I start talking about fudged mercury readings. And we'll keep a closer eye on him now—see if he makes any revealing moves. Put the screws on him without arresting him—yet." Vaughn seemed to be thinking out loud, plotting the scope of his investigation. I didn't dare interrupt him.

But he was ready to change the subject. His tone of voice lightened. "Mainly, I stopped by to let you know I found your stalker. And you were right. It's a woman."

I turned to find his brown eyes gazing at me thoughtfully. "Really?" I couldn't help grinning.

"Stephanie Moreno, who decided that now was a propitious time to fly home and visit her parents in Ames, Iowa. Left her navy-blue, dented Honda Accord in the airport long-term parking lot. But she was fairly forthcoming when I finally got her on the phone. Reiterated that she never meant to scare you."

I wanted to assert that I had never been scared, but that wasn't quite true. *Unnerved* would have been a better description, maybe. "Let me guess," I said instead, "she had an affair with Ian."

The forceful sound Vaughn made this time was a cross between a snort and a grunt. "It appears that Ian used an army of women to collect data, to infiltrate enemy positions, so to speak. He cultivated whistle-blowers within businesses he thought were polluting, and they were usually women. In his world, very often the romantic was tangled up with the activism, the personal with the political." Vaughn sighed again. "Messy."

It was my turn to grunt. "But she didn't work for Cox and Associates."

Vaughn shook his head. "She was an office manager at some outfit called Rocket Shredding which does metal recycling. But she went kayaking with Ian sometimes, and would help him check the sensors. Initially, she thought his obsession with mercury readings was just a hobby. Claims she didn't realize the extent of his motives until after he turned up dead. And then when his death was announced as a murder, she got scared."

"But why didn't she deliver the reports directly to you?" I asked.

"Ahh." Vaughn's mood was improving. He tilted his lopsided grin at me. "She'd helped herself to items of a personal nature at a Walgreens and at the Fred Meyer store in Scappoose on at least five different occasions. She thought—and rightly so—that that string of misdemeanors would affect her credibility."

I had no pithy comment to offer. But I was beginning to feel guilty about the monumental task facing Cal and Willow in the kitchen, so I pushed to my feet. I also wanted to make sure the majority of the leftovers were packed properly and sent home with Cal.

Vaughn followed me inside through the French doors, and we passed through my bedroom without speaking. I hadn't had a chance to do any tidying, so it still appeared as though there'd been a gas main explosion in a Salvation Army thrift store. I tried to pretend it didn't bother me as I tripped on the attached belt of a peach-colored silk shift dress. Vaughn's hand closed quickly around my elbow, and my dignity reasserted itself.

I plunged into helping with kitchen cleanup, turning the tight galley space into sardine-level companionship. Which also left Vaughn standing awkwardly on the other side of the peninsula counter as an observer. But Willow and Cal had been remarkably efficient, and I soon produced a stack of airtight containers laden with food—my meager thank-you offerings for Cal's rescue. For that incident which *could not be mentioned in present company.*

Cal grinned at my discomfiture and juggled the containers into an easy armload. Shocking me out of all sensibility, he leaned in and pecked me on the cheek. "It's been a pleasure, *ma chérie,*" he whispered, affecting both a perfect French accent and a wink. "I'd say we're even now."

Behind me, Willow giggled, followed by one of her snorts. A really loud, dubious snort meant largely for dramatic effect, and probably a commentary on my kayaking ineptitude, not to mention my nosiness. I cringed and flushed heat spread up my cheeks all the way to my hairline. I fired a warning glance at her. We were like a pantomime troupe for revealing secrets.

Vaughn took it all in stride with that little tilted smile of his. But he spared me further embarrassment by not asking any questions. He just gave me a slight nod and followed Cal out. Willow scooted around me and let herself out too, leaving me alone with the dishwasher whooshing quietly in the background.

CHAPTER 18

I called Sloane and vented my recent woes—and reliefs, especially regarding the harmless stalker. As usual, she was the voice of reason and good cheer. We made plans.

The next morning, I trundled garbage bags full of my worst offenders on the stiff-and-stuffy-suit-esque sliding clothing scale up to the parking lot and loaded them into the back of her minivan. Three trips' worth.

I'd brutally followed the 80/20 rule in my selections, keeping only the twenty percent of all my clothes that I would actually wear in my new situation.

Sloanie filled me in as she navigated morning rush hour. She'd scored us coveted chaperone positions for the second-grade's class tour of Franz Bakery due to a wave of influenza that was already decimating the usual herd of mother class helpers. My niece, Ginger, was in the first grade, and so not quite eligible (kids had to be at least seven years old in order to go on the tour), but Sloanie informed me that she'd been finagling spots on the annual tours with the second grade since Ginger had been in preschool.

An elementary-school field trip that the adults fought over? This I had to see. Yet all I could imagine was running around frantically trying to keep wriggly little people from falling into vats of suffocating dough. Not a pretty prospect.

Sloane zipped through town and got us to the school and signed in with time to spare. Three second-grade classes—close to seventy kids—were milling around in front of the school's wide entrance where two bright-yellow buses idled. Their little heads bobbed about mid-thigh height to me. It was a cacophony sea of arguing, singing, laughing, taunting, twirling, spitting, forming up into wobbly lines, with a few of them facing backward and staring at the sky as if they'd rather be anywhere else but there. Already my ears hurt. Sloane patted my arm and gave me a bolstering smile above the noise.

I figured out what the appeal was about two blocks from our destination. It was the scent. Warm, yeasty, moist, wheaty goodness filtered in through the steamed-up bus windows before the driver pulled to a stop.

It even affected the children. They quieted down except for the occasional sniffled complaint about being hungry. They lifted their noses into the air and gazed at each other in wonder.

Once we'd all assembled inside, there was a short history lesson which included some astronomical numbers tallying the weights of various ingredients the bakery used on an annual basis. The kids probably didn't grasp the magnitude of the bakery's operation, but I was duly impressed. We were issued white paper hats and instructed to stay between the yellow lines. From then on, it was a whir of machinery on a massive scale. I'd been right about the vats—or troughs—of dough. There were mixers big enough for three men to fit inside, and giant furnace-type ovens, and conveyor belts overhead that transported phalanxes of hamburger buns on their way to be sliced and packaged.

The kids were in dreamy awe, and required very little minding. Sloanie and I were stationed at the rear, in order to encourage the little dawdlers along, but I found that I was gawking just as much as they were. At the end, we were fed a snack—bread and butter, of course.

But the very best part? Samples—a large paper grocery sack full of various Franz products per adult. Sloane flashed me a triumphant thumbs-up from across the room, and I chuckled with glee.

Loot! I sensed a thick, custardy bread pudding studded with dried apricots and golden raisins in my near future. Maybe with rum sauce? Mmmm. Comfort food at its finest.

We did have to listen to the kids singing the jingle, "Franz bread, the good bread, flavor beyond compare!" over and over again all the way back to the school, but it was worth it.

When we got back to the *Tin Can* (which Sloanie snickered over), we decided on a long walk—a sort of preemptive strike against the calories we knew we'd be consuming once we unpacked the baked goods. Besides, the wildlife refuge and the crisp turning-into-autumn air beckoned. It was also one more opportunity for me to avoid the reality that I really needed to find more jobs.

We did what we do best—shared each other's company without talking. Just being. How I'd missed her. The rustle of dry leaves under our feet and the dappled sunlight reinforced the companionable peacefulness of our trek.

"Tell me honestly," she said after close to a mile of long, thoughtful silence. "Are you glad you moved here?"

We'd reached the riverbank, our toes sinking into the wet sandy ledge left by the receding tide.

"Are you kidding?" I turned to her with wide eyes that immediately welled up. "More than I can say." I wrapped her in a tight hug. "More than I can say," I repeated into her hair.

"I guess some things haven't changed," she murmured with a smile, pulling away a few inches in order to study me closely. "People still talk to you. It's your special talent—absorbing other people's confidences. I'd just hoped that you wouldn't be overwhelmed with an entirely new set of acquaintances. But I guess this level of involvement isn't something you could leave behind—it's an intrinsic thing with you."

"Do you mean Bettina? Or are you referring to my meddlesomeness in general?" I frowned.

"No, silly." She shook her head. "I mean all of them—Bettina, Willow, this guy Cal, even Roxy. I think that detective, too, in his own way. He keeps showing up to talk to you." She nudged me with her elbow. "Ever wonder why?"

A great blue heron chose that moment to relieve himself into the water from a low branch about ten feet away. Splat! I jumped about a mile. I hadn't even noticed the lurking mass of dingy slate-blue feathers tucked into the tree. He extended his long neck and *braaack*ed an obnoxious squawk as though announcing that his major feat for the day had been accomplished. He eyed us for a moment and ruffled himself back into a relaxed hunker.

Sloane snorted. "On that note, I should be heading home. Grey will be up from his second nap soon, and I need to relieve the babysitter before she pulls her hair out."

Sloane came into the *Tin Can* just for a moment to visit the loo before her drive home. I took the opportunity to inventory the contents of my Franz sample bag. But when I walked Sloane to the front door to say good-bye, we were accosted by Bettina, her fist raised, on the verge of knocking.

The ends of Bettina's neatly bobbed hair were flipped out in frazzled directions, and her face was alarmingly pale. She flashed a wan, habitually polite smile at Sloane, but gripped my arm so hard I winced. "I'm going to lose my nerve. You have to come tomorrow night." Then she marched inside, straight for the kitchen and the French press.

"What did I tell you?" Sloane whispered. "Intrinsic. You're an irresistible magnet for people who need to spill their own beans." But she said it with a grin and one knowingly lifted eyebrow and gave me a good-luck flit of her fingers before she slipped away.

~oOo~

I was supposed to be drumming up more work. Focus. Concentrate. Apply myself diligently like the good little entrepreneur I was hoping to be. Yeah, right.

It's just that when you have the lurking threat of an undercover sting operation looming over you, it's a little hard to pay appropriate attention to the more mundane aspects of life.

Which meant I cooked up a storm instead of engaging in schmoozing under the guise of networking. And, having no one else to inflict the results of my stress flurry upon, I knocked on the *Ecclesiastes'* hull once again.

"What's this?" Cal asked when he emerged. His gaze was fastened on the warm baking pan I was cradling in its potholder nest against my chest.

"I want to make a deposit against future services—and advice."

He blinked, then grinned, then held out his arms. "Okay."

When I handed over the bread pudding, he just about stuck his nose in the custard, inhaling deeply.

"Got any tips for me?" I asked. "I presume you know about Bettina's harebrained scheme. I can't believe that detective is going along with it."

"Karleen Jett?" Cal brightened, his blue eyes glittering with amusement. "That girl's got balls, for sure. Yeah, I know," he added more somberly. "Don't worry. Karleen will have everything lined up perfectly. Your job is to keep Bettina from freaking out."

"Terrific," I moaned.

It had taken two hours of coffee, brioche, and talking to restore Bettina to some semblance of confidence in her own ability to act normal under pressure. If we had one thing going for us, it was that Norman didn't have much experience with what was normal behavior for Bettina since they'd only had one in-person date. Chatting on Facebook didn't count in this context, a fact I had reminded Bettina of over and over again.

In the process, I'd revealed more of the digital high jinks I'd performed for my last employer than I'd intended to, but the fresh information had seemed to set Bettina's mind at ease. I was worried she now viewed me as an expert in cybercrime. She didn't fully grasp that I'd been on the (legally?) perpetrating side of the equation, not the solving side.

I checked my watch. The plan was for Willow and me to be in the restaurant before Bettina showed up with Norman. Karleen—whom I had yet to meet—was going to be there too. I'd purposely skipped breakfast and lunch, knowing I would have to make a good showing of eating at the restaurant and not give the waitress a reason to hurry us out before the operation was completed.

I wasn't altogether sure my stomach was up to the task of eating for effect, because Norman, in his current state of thriftiness, had chosen the local franchise of a casual-dining chain of restaurants which shall remain nameless. But you'd know the name if I told you, and it was the type of business that had never had a reputation for anything other than greasy breakfasts (made with the kind of grade-B eggs that come already scrambled in five-gallon buckets) served all day and at record speed. High turnover was the name of the game. I couldn't imagine how Norman could clinch the deal in such a nonconducive environment, but that was his problem, not mine.

It was time to get ready. Fortunately, I only needed to look like a road-weary traveler with an undiscerning palate.

CHAPTER 19

"I'm sorry Roxy couldn't make it," I said to Willow as we pulled into the restaurant parking lot.

In her final tizzy before we had to leave her alone at *Dock's End* so Norman could unsuspectingly pick her up, Bettina had decided that more would be merrier. By that point, embarrassment over her gullibility had been replaced with the need to be surrounded by supportive friends. Which meant she'd also brought Roxy up to speed while simultaneously demanding that, as the marina manager, she permanently ban Norman from marina property—after the sting was over, of course.

I had no idea how Roxy could enforce such a restriction, but she'd promised without reservation. She had, however, declined the invitation to dinner.

"It's the smoking," Willow said, turning to me, her face scrunched with worry. "She's killing herself, you know. She can't go five minutes without a cigarette which rules out going pretty much anywhere in public. She'll drive me places in the car, but she won't actually go inside with me." Her tone was mournful. "Like this"—she pointed at the gigantic poster of a cinnamon roll hung in the restaurant's plate glass window—"it's a treat for me to be taken out to eat by someone I like, have a conversation about whatever, you know? But Gran would never..." She shrugged and quickly looked out the side window.

What a loss. I desperately wanted to reach over and hug her, but I wasn't yet sure how she'd respond to a physical display of affection. I didn't think she was getting much of that at home either—which made her budding boy-crush thing all the more worrisome. Because she probably would end up seeking affection at some point, and since her options were limited, she might go after an illusory, abusive source out of desperation. The poor kid.

Worse yet, I didn't have any consoling answers for her. I set the Volvo's emergency brake and opened my door. "Game on," I said instead. "Ready for incognito?"

Willow snorted. She'd opted to wear her newsboy cap because it completely covered her blue hair. She looked like an anemic wraith in an oversized grunge band t-shirt and her favorite ripped jeans.

I tried to channel the inner musings that the mother of such a child ought to be experiencing, but I was having trouble mustering anything coherent. I settled on being grateful that she wasn't too embarrassed to be seen with me, for I, too, had on a hat—a giant, floppy sun hat wrapped with a fuchsia bow which Bettina had lent me for the occasion. It was slightly large for me, so I couldn't imagine how it must overwhelm her tiny frame when she wore it. But our ridiculous get-ups would enable Bettina to spot us from wherever she and Norman happened to get seated in the restaurant, so I'd consented to the contrivance.

I guess we were lucky. The hostess immediately showed us to an open booth, right next to the entrance. Every time the door opened, a blast of climate-controlled air whirled around us, bringing the chill of unnecessary air conditioning. But there was no way we'd miss Bettina or she'd miss us.

We were paging through the laminated menus, sticky from all the fingers before ours, when Willow kicked me square in the shin. I bit my tongue but still couldn't suppress a groan.

Bettina and her pseudo-amore breezed past us on their way to a corner booth. Norman was even taller than I remembered—probably because I was seeing him from a normal sitting height this time instead of from river level. He had his hand spread across the middle of Bettina's back in a most proprietary manner. She was doing a great job of not visibly cringing.

I sipped ice water and debated between a Reuben sandwich and a Cobb salad. Willow was studying the pictures of gooey chocolate and ice cream concoctions on the dessert page with an intensity that ought to be reserved for subjects like ancient Greek philosophy or calculus.

It was my turn to kick her under the table. "One green thing," I muttered. "At least one. Even if it's only a pickle spear garnish." My token mother-ism for the day.

Willow snorted and flipped back to the senior citizen specials—all of which ought to come with a side of Metamucil at this particular franchise, I thought. A moment later, her gray eyes were flashing at me from across the table. "There, there—there!" she hissed with a jerk of her chin.

I swiveled surreptitiously to see an older couple being led into the restaurant's other wing. The woman put up a subdued but insistent fuss about something, and the hostess swung around to lead them into our section.

Willow gave me a knowing grin. "Detective Jett." She shrugged. "Don't know who the guy is, though. She was divorced ages ago. Maybe she has a new boyfriend too."

After more disgruntled pointing toward the ceiling vents and stern shakes of her head, Detective Jett got the hostess to concede a center table set for four potential diners kitty-corner from Bettina's booth. With a scraping of chairs and noisy rustling, Detective Jett and her date claimed their seats and ordered coffee.

From my vantage point, I could tell that Norman was already yakking Bettina's ear off. I knew Detective Jett had coached her on specific things she needed to hear from Norman, particular phrasing that would serve as incontrovertible evidence in court. Bettina was going to have to play dumb in order to get him to lay out the details of his plan again—and especially what he was promising in return for her investment—in the most basic language. If she could get him to produce a contract, that would be a coup d'état.

I supposed my audio recording could be used as a backup, but it hadn't been taken with anyone's consent, so it would present a tricky legal problem. Detective Jett was right to want Norman's deceit and fraudulent motives laid out as cleanly as possible.

Norman's upper half was tilted way over the table as he tried to persuade Bettina. She leaned back and scowled at him, which made him stretch even farther, his long fingers drawing imaginary profits on the tabletop as he made his point. His body language, the pressure he was applying—all spoke to his desperation. He was way beyond the soft-sell stage.

And from all appearances, Bettina was performing superbly. Her obvious reluctance was drawing Norman out more and more. I didn't know what she'd been worried about. Once, as the waitress was plunking our plates on the table, I caught her eye across the room and gave her an approving nod. She just scowled harder and fiddled with a sugar packet. Attagirl—string him along.

"Gimme the play-by-play." Willow stuffed three French fries in her mouth and waved the lettuce leaf from her burger at me in an obliging gesture. "I'm dying here." She'd sneaked a few peeks over the back of the booth earlier, but she was doing a remarkable job of not blowing our cover. Although, frankly, I doubted Norman was paying much attention to anything other than his lonely-widow prey.

"He certainly has the gift of gab. Oh, wait," I said, sitting up straighter for a better view. "Ah-ha. He just slid a leather notebook onto the table, and he's wiping it with his sleeve. Probably got maple syrup on it. Now he's opening it—slowly—there are papers inside. He's poking at the papers—talking—now he closed it again." I huffed and slumped against the vinyl cushion. My Reuben no longer looked appetizing. I shook my head and swirled the ice in my glass. "More talking. Bettina's stabbing her steak like it's not already dead and cooked. I think she ordered the most expensive thing on the menu. He must have said something that made her especially mad."

"Geez. What a blowhard." Willow squeezed an upturned ketchup bottle, and it spluttered disgusting red droplets all over her T-shirt instead of on her plate where she'd been aiming it.

I handed her my napkin. "The notebook's open again. He's hardly touched his food, but Bettina's polishing off her broccoli now, which is saying something." I love food, including most green things—my earlier order to Willow hadn't been hypocritical—but broccoli is one cruciferous vegetable that has never wormed its way into my good opinion. Uniformly avoiding it is probably the only matter of policy I'd ever agreed with former president George Bush the Elder about.

"There it is," I whispered excitedly. "He's pulling out a few papers now, gesturing with his pen—looks like...looks like...yes! Bettina's pulled the papers over to her side of the table. She's chewing on the pen cap. She's blotting something with her napkin, asking a question...Norman looks like he's going to pop a vein. Yes! She's signing!"

"Really?" Willow squealed and snuck a gander of her own around the edge of the booth.

Yes, indeed. Bettina finished her signature with what appeared to be a big curlicue and an emphatic stab of the pen. Yes, indeed. At some point—I'd missed it earlier—she'd fished her checkbook out of her purse, and it lay on the table beside the signed document. Now she held the cover open with the pen poised to add her signature on that bottom line too.

Over at Detective Jett's table, her man friend was also signing something—in a whisking, cramped scrawl. I could imagine the sound of the pen grating across the paper on the hard surface of the table as he hurried. And then Detective Jett was on her feet and muscling in on Norman's ill-concealed celebration.

She didn't say much—just a few terse commands from the look of it—but he shot out of his seat as though he'd just realized it was infested with lice. Just as quickly, Detective Jett reached up, twisted a handful of his collar, and tapped the back of his knee with the toe of her spit-shined, lace-up shoe. He dropped onto the booth bench, squirming and flushed, but pinned firmly in place. Detective Jett was a sturdy woman with a low center of gravity, and she wasn't budging.

My phone rang. Talk about inconvenient timing. I dug it out of my purse and answered it quickly before the ringing annoyed our fellow diners. Fortunately, most of the customers in our section of the restaurant were only just becoming aware—in a vague, irritated sort of way—of the minor scuffle in the corner.

"Oh, my gosh," Lila breathed into my ear. "Frank's been arrested!"

I blinked and frowned at the cluster of people at Bettina's booth. I could just barely see a bit of her orange hair behind the broad backs of Detective Jett and her date. Then a couple uniformed cops entered on a blast of scorched-grease-scented air and strode past our table. Willow's eyes were huge.

"Um, well, I guess that's expected," I mumbled into the phone, even though I was rather surprised. Vaughn had given every indication that he was going to let Frank Cox dangle while waiting to see what other evidence might turn up. "Standard procedure," I added for good measure while craning my neck to keep track of the happenings in the corner. It was a regular party back there.

"I mean, I thought he was so aboveboard, so pristine," Lila continued. "Frank's terribly conscientious about the environment; it's just that he has business interests to attend to as well. He and Ian didn't always see eye-to-eye, but murder? I didn't really believe it," she said in a hushed, dramatic stage whisper. "And I slept with him."

Ahh, so *that* was the problem. I could see how it would be. "Innocent until proven guilty." The words tumbled out of my mouth automatically—just for something to say while I scooted to the end of the bench and tried to figure out what was going on with Bettina and Norman. Everyone in the corner, cops included, was standing in a tight huddle with their backs to us, and while they had to be discussing something, I couldn't gather any hints as to the content of the conversation.

"Yes, of course," Lila agreed. "Just have to carry on, right? Speaking of which, I have another job for you. Interested?"

"Yeah, sure," I mumbled. One of the cops had just removed a pair of handcuffs from his belt. Willow was bouncing on the bench opposite me, emitting little squeaks and pointing. I flapped a hand at her to indicate that, yes, I'd seen that flash of silvery metal too.

"Can you meet me at Peregrine Pointe in the morning? At nine?"

"Yeah." I fumbled in my purse for something to write with.

"Looks like one of Frank's contractors is going to take over the operation since Frank's preoccupied at the moment. They're almost ready to draw up pre-lease agreements with future tenants. Just up your alley—lining up the right mix of retail and service businesses, promoting the property, et cetera. I'm very impressed with how you're handling the launch of the Wicked Bean Annex. Everyone was talking about the soft opening at the office yesterday." Lila was rambling now, in a forced, upbeat tone.

"Right," I muttered, but my eyes were glued to the satisfying sight of Norman being placed in handcuffs.

His face was livid—the shade of a fresh, nasty bruise—and his jaw muscles were bulging. One of the cops recited his Miranda rights in a monotone. I couldn't hear all the words, but the cadence was unmistakable.

Norman appeared to be taking his right to remain silent seriously, but everything else about his demeanor screamed fury. To be bested by a tiny, orange-haired lady was an outrageous comeuppance he hadn't anticipated.

"Yeah, yeah," I muttered again to Lila in case I hadn't been making the appropriate comments at the appropriate times. She seemed satisfied and said good-bye.

I dropped my phone back in my purse just as Norman was frog-marched past our table. He wasn't making eye contact with anyone, though, so I'm afraid Willow and I gaped openly, along with all of the other patrons. Who knew rubbery salads and all-day biscuits and gravy would come with a cops-and-robbers floor show?

"Oh, girls. Oh, my." Bettina arrived breathless, with a hand pressed against the layers of necklaces strung across her sternum. "Whew." She slid onto the bench beside Willow.

Plan A had been that we were her ride home. I was so pleased we hadn't needed to explore Plan B or C or more.

I shoved my sandwich out of the way and leaned forward. "Who's that man with Detective Jett?"

Bettina chuckled. "Judge Riker. He's on arrest warrant duty this week. He likes to get in on the action once in a while." She rolled her eyes. "He'll recuse himself if the case happens to go to court and it happens to get assigned to him. To each his own, but I guess he gets bored sitting behind his bench all the time. Goodness knows, that was an excitement I could well do without, but Karleen puts up with his quirks. Anyway, he got to witness firsthand that scoundrel trying to bilk me out of my retirement money."

"You were awesome." Willow flung an arm around Bettina's shoulders and squeezed.

"Here, here." I lifted my water glass in salute. "The contract's not enforceable, is it?"

"Nope. It's now safely in Karleen's possession. She'll log it in as evidence." Bettina patted her purse. "And my nest egg's safe too." She exhaled and relaxed against the seat, a wide smile lightening her face for the first time in days.

But there was an inkling of something else in her warm brown eyes—a glint that tweaked a little bolt of worry through my chest cavity and left me panting. I got the distinct impression that Bettina had enjoyed herself immensely, her protestations otherwise notwithstanding, that she might have just become addicted to a certain type of adrenaline surge.

This did not bode well. Especially not if she expected me to continue being the holder of her secrets.

CHAPTER 20

The sound of rain splattering on the tin roof woke me early the next morning. It was a fabulous sound, especially since I knew the exterior of my house was freshly up to snuff. I had just snuggled down deeper under the duvet for a few more minutes of shut-eye when I remembered what day it was—Wednesday.

I flew out of bed, pulled on a sweat suit, and dashed through the rain to a newspaper box that was chained to a post outside a convenience store down the road and picked up a free copy of *Willamette Week*. I stuffed it under my jacket and trotted home, along the way also refreshing my memory about the reasons why I rarely (never) jog. I splashed through puddles the size of kiddie pools. From the looks of things, it had been raining all night, and there were no signs that the heavy, pewter-gray cloud cover was going to dissipate anytime soon.

Josie hadn't been exaggerating about the amount of space the editor had deemed necessary to dedicate to Ian Thorpe's life, passing, and manner of death. Someone on the newspaper's staff had dredged up a collection of pictures, assembling what amounted to a centerfold of Ian Thorpe's greatest accomplishments.

And I had to admit that particular staff member was really good at her job. She (or he?—but why did I have a suspicion that anyone who so lovingly curated a pictorial history of Ian was a *she*?) certainly hadn't taken the path of least resistance since more than half of the photos were new to me—pictures which had *not* been available on the various websites I'd visited while doing my own research on the activist. I settled, cross-legged and with my hair still dripping, on the yoga mat, ignored my usual exercise regimen, and read the captions.

In the bottom left corner, among the most recently dated photos, I spotted a familiar face. Lila Halton, her blonde hair flying loose around her shoulders while she huddled against Ian in a group shot. Everyone was bundled for inclement weather, and they were posed on the edge of a cliff or something, because the scenery behind them was distant and probably would have been spectacular if the picture had been printed in four-color instead of the more economical black ink only. They were a happy bunch, celebrating a trust fund purchase of a chunk of Columbia River frontage property and thereby saving it from the evils of a proposed oil terminal, according to the caption.

It wouldn't surprise me if a crop of parks, funds, scholarships, and greenways sprung up in the near future, all bearing, in memorial, the name of our illustrious Ian Thorpe. He sure looked good on promotional materials.

Having completed that rabbit trail, I flipped through the entertainment section to my real reason for rushing out to the get the paper—to see what kind of write-up Josie had done for the Wicked Bean Annex. I nodded appreciatively as I read. The girl had an extensive vocabulary at her disposal and used it to masterful effect. I mentally bumped her up in my Rolodex list. She could get the job done, with style.

And then I had to hurry. I was getting slack in my entrepreneurialism. But wasn't nine a.m. kind of early for a business meeting?

~oOo~

I'd had to search for Peregrine Pointe online to find out where it was. Took me forever to figure out there was an *e* on the end of *Pointe*, too. I could have called Lila to double-check, but that would have appeared as though I hadn't been paying attention during her phone call—during Norman's arrest—which was exactly the case. I just didn't want to admit it.

Turned out I didn't have to drive far. And that Peregrine Pointe was a very long way from living up to its name. It was the former Cox and Associates development just south, and upriver, from the wildlife refuge. I could have walked there, but I'd expended all my aerobic effort for the day, and I was running late. I slowed the Volvo to a crawl and gripped the steering wheel tighter as my old battleship slid on the muddy track leading into the property. The windshield wipers sounded like someone was trying to tune up a washtub bass.

The pre-lease agreements for Peregrine Pointe must have been based on blueprints, because there was a whole lot of nothing except mud, a few concrete pillars, and slipshod rows of black silt fencing at the site. All the earthmoving equipment I'd seen on my brief kayak tour was gone. I parked next to the only shelter, a construction trailer, and alongside the only other car on the property, a sporty little Subaru.

Lila had the door of the construction trailer open by the time I'd slogged over to the steps. "Welcome," she said with a wry laugh. "Now that you're having an up-close-and-personal experience with the notorious Pacific Northwest rain, are you sure you're glad you moved here?"

I chuckled and tried to scrape the mud off my heels on the top stair tread before entering. It was not the sort of facility that had a welcome mat on the doorstep.

"It only gets worse," she added. "Fall, winter, and spring are all equally wet."

"I'll survive." I plunked my tote bag on a spare metal folding chair and fished out the supplies I'd need.

The office was in a state of disarray that might or might not have been normal. I imagined whoever usually worked in this space didn't have the time or inclination for general housekeeping and paperwork management. But the trailer had the basic necessities—a few flat surfaces to spread out on, a bunch of chairs, a space heater, a coffeemaker perched on a low bookcase, and a bottled-water stand in the corner.

Lila had already set up on a plastic-topped, folding conference table that was decorated with dried coffee rings and blue ink marks. "Feels eerie, huh?" She perched on the edge of her chair and crossed her legs, her manner all business. "Usually can't hear yourself think around here for all the back-up beeping and big machinery shoving dirt around. But Joe Vanderpoole will be on it in no time. Of course, he has to work through an extra layer of lawyers now that Frank's in jail. That makes signing contracts tricky, but this place will be buzzing again by the end of next week at the latest." She tapped the touchpad on her laptop, and her eyes roved back and forth across whatever appeared on the screen as she continued talking as only an experienced multitasker can do. The stylishly-retro, teal-framed glasses were not in attendance this morning, but that didn't seem to affect her ability to read. "So he doesn't want to waste any time in signing up potential tenants. The bank wants to see future income projections that have something to back them up."

I nodded and scribbled notes. Banks were picky that way. "Seems fast," I commented, thinking aloud about all the legal and financial hoops a rapid ownership change for a property currently under development would require.

"Ross is going to lean on the county commissioners, get the permits moving on this place. Shouldn't be a problem." Lila was pecking at her keyboard, still absorbed by the information on her screen.

My own hands froze, hovering over my notepad. The city councilman's name alone gave me the chills—the creepy, bad-omen kind. "Wait. Ross Perkins is involved in this? We're not inside Portland city limits here."

Lila peered at me over her laptop's monitor, her hazel eyes wide. "Since when did those kinds of boundaries stop Ross? His brother-in-law is one of the subcontractors on this project. I don't love his involvement either, but he's anxious to provide jobs and improve the economic health of the region, even beyond the city." She was so smooth, so matter-of-fact, so ready with the good-intentions veneer. "You have to pick your priorities, and right now a prime development that's stuck in a quagmire of bureaucracy is far worse than one that is proceeding on schedule and destined to add to the county's tax coffers."

This revelation made my entire digestive tract shrivel into sinewy knots. My revulsion probably also showed on my face.

"No." I snapped my notebook shut. I'd assumed this new job would be Frank Cox- and Ross Perkins-free because of the new ownership. Unfortunately, the sleazy connection tendrils were pervasive and unrelenting. I pushed my chair back and stood.

"No?" Lila's forehead was lined with confusion.

I thought I'd explained clearly when I'd quit the last time. Why should she be surprised that I quit before I started this time since the circumstances were ethically similar? Unless she'd told me about the murky provenance of this job last night and I'd been too distracted to catch the full meaning while watching Norman's demise.

"No," I said again, more emphatically. "I would rather starve. I should never have spread my business cards around City Hall. If you ever have a job that doesn't include a politician or someone on a politician's undeclared payroll, *then* I'd be interested."

"Don't you understand?" Lila stood now too, and slowly closed her laptop. Her fingertips rested lightly on the table on either side of the computer, but her gaze was solidly on me, her hazel eyes hard and appraising. "Sometimes you have to join them to beat them."

Something was pinging around in the back of my brain. Neurons were flirting with each other—they hadn't hooked up yet, but they would. I closed my eyes for just a moment and inhaled. It was best if I didn't get in my brain's way at moments like this. So I took the tactical step of silence. Patience always pays off.

Lila was studying me, her body tense all except for those fingertips which were still resting lightly. Her lips twitched—no sound—but I could tell that it was a warm-up movement, and that I was going to win this particular out-silencing bout in record time.

But she didn't say anything. Her eyes grew flinty, narrower. Her nostrils flared, just the tiniest bit. And then the fingertips pressed into the table until they were white.

It hit me with all the subtlety of a wallop. I might have even flinched. Amazing how a thought can have a physical impact.

If Lila had been telling the truth last night and Frank had been arrested, then Vaughn had a really good reason to do so. And that would have meant that the timing—placing Frank and Ian together at some point near Ian's estimated time of death—worked, which would also mean that Frank's alibi didn't hold up. And since Lila had been Frank's alibi, then she had to be in question now too. Had she been sleeping on both sides of the fence?

I was no longer certain silence was the best option.

I slipped my notebook into my tote bag and casually slung the bag over my shoulder. "You know," I said, "I read the *Willamette Week* this morning. They printed a really good picture of you and Ian all cozy-like at a function earlier this year. A party, really. A celebration. You two were an item. Did he dump you too, once your usefulness wore out?" It was an allegation—a stretch, but not a very big one, considering.

Lila maintained her speechlessness, but her response was more than enough answer. I'd thought maybe she'd burst into tears. Wasn't that what women did when they were heartbroken? Given our history of late-night girl-talk sessions, I was expecting more of the same maudlin melodrama.

But not little Lila, not when confronted in the flesh. She launched herself over the table and was clawing at me before I had a chance to realize that what I was seeing was reality and not some bizarre hallucination.

I raised my tote bag just in time and shoved it against her chest. It weighs a ton, but as a shield it's not terribly effective. I dropped it, and it landed on her foot.

While she was hopping and screaming, "You don't understand!" I pulled open the door to the trailer and skidded out onto the top step.

Mud. Slick mud from my earlier shoe-scraping.

I was still mostly upright when I landed at the bottom of the stairs, but then Lila was on me like a piggyback rider, kicking her sharp heels into my sides, a forearm clamped across my neck. I bent in half, collapsed my face into my knees (there's something to be said for practicing a yoga ritual nearly every morning), and she slid off head-first into more mud.

I didn't stick around. I had our two cars between us before she'd righted herself and swiped her hair back out of her eyes.

I thought maybe I could reason with her. You know, talk like civilized adults? Plus, my car keys were in my tote bag. What did I care if she'd been two-timing a couple of guys who hated one another's guts? Or even if one of them had set her up to tattle on the other one's activities?

"I understand if you thought it was necessary to spy on Frank Cox for Ian by dating him," I offered. "Or working for him," I added since I couldn't remember which aspect had come first, or if the sequence mattered.

"You don't understand!" Lila screamed again. This was getting monotonous.

"Why don't you explain it to me?" I wanted to say the words calmly, but Lila was picking her way around the back of her car. I sounded a little short of breath as I sidled sideways, keeping the full width and weight of my old tank of a car between us and accumulating gloppy layers of mud on my boots in the process.

"He loved me," Lila announced and raised a fist full of clenched keys.

As a weapon, she'd have to throw the clump of jangling metal, so I wasn't too worried. Besides I needed clarification. "Which he?" I asked.

Lila stabbed a key into the lock on the trunk of her car and popped the lid open. "Ian," she grunted, completely hidden behind the tiny hatch. She emerged with a kayak paddle.

I was mystified as to how the paddle had fit. Maybe the engineer who designed the vehicle put a premium on cargo space over leg room. Another reason I would never drive a sports car.

"What about Frank?" The pieces still weren't fitting together in my head—at least not well enough to explain why Lila would go berserk like this.

"Complete and utter idiot." Lila snorted in a way that would have made Willow proud.

I knew her statement couldn't be entirely true. Frank had figured out how to hire a teenage hacker. Not without leaving a trail, but still, that's not something most people would consider doing. Most people also weren't motivated by the prospect of massive fines for polluting a public waterway, either—if Ian's mercury readings were correct and came to the attention of the proper officials.

"So you should be glad Frank's facing the tough questions down at the police station then," I said. "Right? Considering your feelings for Ian."

"Except for one teensy problem." Lila advanced, the paddle balanced easily in her right hand. "Frank might be tempted to tell the whole truth."

It had dawned on me that a kayak paddle wasn't particularly useful for navigating muddy construction sites. But it might make a sufficient...what was a name of a weapon which an attacker used to whack someone else upside the head? Bludgeon? Thumper? Cranium-cracker? The paddle was plastic, not too heavy, but wielded at the right angle, it could be vicious. She wasn't swinging it yet, but I didn't plan on letting her get close enough to try it, either.

"It'll be expensive," I agreed, backing up.

Lila faltered, her gaze locked onto me, the skin of her face so taut she reminded me of an aging actress who'd had too many plastic surgeries.

"What?" I bleated. I didn't dare risk a glance over my shoulder to get my bearings.

"Expensive?" She took another step forward.

"The pollution. Fines." I waved a hand indicating the muddy acreage we were in the midst of. "I assume the digging here has exposed toxic soil that's leaching, or else Frank has been dumping contaminated materials from one of his other sites on this riverbank to reinforce it, carve himself a little more real estate so he can build right to the edge of the river. The mercury readings have been elevated..." I trailed off because Lila had developed large, ugly red blotches on her cheeks and neck.

She hadn't known about the sensors. Her soaring blood pressure and hollow stare made that clear.

I'd assumed that any woman who'd slept with Ian also knew about all his pet projects. Big mistake. I should have realized the man had been able to compartmentalize better than that.

Then what was Lila worried that Frank might blab about? The other big thing was the murder. Why shouldn't Frank confess to both in one fell swoop?

Unless.

Unless he was responsible for only one of the crimes. Massive fines were nothing compared to a murder rap.

What did Frank know?

At least he was safe inside a jail cell or an interrogation room. I was standing in the mucky middle of nowhere facing off with a crazy woman. My phone was in my tote bag along with my keys.

The accelerating effects of adrenaline on the brain are amazing. I'd processed a lot of causation versus correlation analysis in about the same amount of time it took for Lila to shift her weight. Enough for me to consider her far more dangerous than her petite size might otherwise suggest.

She shot forward like a drag racer at the drop of the flag. I didn't bother with parrying or feinting—I turned and fled. My legs were longer than hers.

It was like one of those horrible dreams where you're running in slow motion no matter how much blood-pounding effort you put into the excruciating sprint. Plod. Drag. Plod. Drag. Each of my feet gained about a pound of mud with every awkward stride.

I glanced back. Lila weighed less than I did, and it was proving to be an advantage. She sort of skimmed over the top while I sank in with each leg thrust.

She tried to hook me from behind with the paddle. I swerved, fell, rolled, and somehow got back on my feet. Set my sights on the river, and a spot where the perimeter silt fence had collapsed. It became my goal, if for no other reason than that it wasn't muddy in the river.

A sharp jab from behind, and a sudden burning pain in the meat of my right thigh. Lila was using the paddle like a spear—stabbing and slicing. She had the technique down pat.

I reached around, grabbed the flat blade on the end of the paddle as it arced toward me on her next pass. It snapped off and left my hand stinging. She'd have to change her lunging motion or take a moment to flip the paddle around. I surged ahead. The fence gap was close—fifteen feet maybe.

This time the shaft of the paddle connected with my back, across my ribs, scraping vertebrae. I stumbled, flung my arms out. Before I could regain my balance, Lila had the shaft between my knees, torquing it. I slipped sideways and crashed into the first jumbled heap of fencing. In the process, I jammed my left foot on a wood stake embedded in the fabric of the fence, and my ankle rolled over with a grisly crackling sound.

So close. I rolled again. There's no claim to fame in crossing the finish line on your feet—as long as you cross the line.

The bank had been elevated and reinforced with a concrete retaining wall to provide a level, buildable surface. I went off the ledge, and the drop felt like interminable minutes of cold nothingness. It couldn't have been more than a fraction of a second though, and then I hit the water, stunning the air out of my lungs.

Breathing, blood pumping, thinking, blinking—it all stopped.

CHAPTER 21

My brain screamed for oxygen and kicked my reflexes into action. I flailed to the surface and gulped a searing breath. Lila was lying on her stomach, gripping the edge of the retaining wall, her hair a wild snarl around her head as she peered down at me.

With a couple sluggish strokes, I extended the gap between us, out of paddle-swinging range. If she wanted to get me now, she'd have to enter the river too, or find a weapon that fired bullets. I tried to blink the water out of my eyes, clear my head, steady my ragged breathing.

She hadn't moved. She wasn't going to come after me. Or was she? I'd read her wrong all along. No reason my track record should improve now.

I kept swimming. Clumsily—my sodden clothing dragged on my limbs. In less than a minute, just staying afloat required all of my energy. It was so cold that I couldn't feel the injuries to my ankle or thigh or back and ribs. Pain was probably raging through my body, but I wasn't registering any sensation other than numbness.

My only consolation was knowing that, due to the current, floaters often ended up at the marina. At least I had a slim chance of being close to home when someone found me. I didn't harbor any illusions that I could stay conscious the whole distance.

I thwacked into something hard then bobbed around a splintered wood piling, its broken top barely poking out of the water. Then another one, a little taller, thick as a telephone pole. I curled and arched and managed to hook my arms around it as the current tugged on my clothing.

There was a lump, a knob on the slippery, algae-slicked wood just below the surface of the water, and I grabbed hold of it. A moment later, my handhold broke free, and so did I. All I had to show for my fumbling efforts was a fistful of cracked plastic and a dangling wire.

I rolled, tried to stay on my back, spread my arms like a snow angel so I could have a view downriver and see what was coming next.

Another long row of decaying pilings. This stretch of river must have been a busy commercial port many decades ago. Maybe the docks had been ferry landings before Portland's bridges had been built, or for unloading cargo of some kind. I swirled my hands, flicked my feet—at least I intended to, but couldn't tell whether they were functioning or not—trying to aim myself. I'd only have one shot at grabbing another piling as I drifted by.

Bear hug. If that piling had been alive, I would have squeezed all the air out of it. Initially, I hadn't latched on so much as been swept into it. The rush of the water pressed me against the rough wood. But then my arms and legs wrapped around it, and nothing ever felt so solid or so good, even if it was coated in green slime.

I dug my fingernails into rotted crevices and banged my knee on a crossbar a couple feet under the surface, which probably linked to the next piling over. With some squirming, I hooked the heel of my right boot on that narrow horizontal ridge—another point of contact. I'd take all of the leech-like connections I could get.

And then it was just a matter of hanging on. I was getting fuzzy, losing focus. How long until someone on a passing boat noticed me? Tugs, barges, leisure craft, maybe a late-season sightseeing outing or a fishing charter? I had to hope someone would spot the weird bump on this particular piling and come investigate.

Hang on. Hang on. Hang on. It became a broken-record mantra in my mind. I pressed my cheek against the black wire stapled vertically up the piling. Which wasn't decades old. Which meant someone, somewhat recently, had visited this piling. Maybe he would return soon.

~oOo~

Small, dark eyes and a broad, squatty nose. And whiskers. Lots of whiskers.

It was so cute and sleek. The creature slipped and dove in the water around me, popping up here and there. And then I realized it wasn't just one—there were several. So acrobatic and busy that I couldn't get a firm count.

Apparently, I was a novelty and a territory invader, and they'd come to check me out. I was in no position to be a threat with my arms and legs clamped around the piling while the rain pelted down around me, creating divots in the swelling river surface. They seemed to sense that my presence was innocuous, that I was unable to help myself, let alone disturb them. They nudged me occasionally while diving, bumped my elbow with a curious nose once, shook droplets from their furry heads when they came up for air, and chirped to each other.

They were adorable, and I was thinking how much I'd like to bring my nieces to see them. Ginger and Hazel would probably squeal with delight, though, and startle the otters.

But since I didn't move, and wasn't currently edible, the otters quickly lost interest and moved on to more productive fishing grounds.

~oOo~

"Eva." Tight ropes cinched my waist. "Eva, honey, let go."

Not ropes. Arms. The voice was warm in my ear.

"Eva. Damn it," Cal said. "I don't want to be making a habit of this."

"Me neither," I murmured, not sure what he was complaining about.

"Let go, then." A hand closed over one of mine, prying at my fingers. "I have you. Come on."

I cracked my eyes open.

"Come on." His face was inches from mine, and there were several bright-yellow nylon ropes looped around both me and the piling. Cal was sitting in a kayak, floating level with me, and the kayak seemed to be lashed to the piling too, because his hands were free. Free to help me.

I might have sobbed a little.

"That's right, honey," Cal said. "Let go. I have you. I know this kayak wasn't built for two, but it'll work. Like riding on the handlebars of a bike."

"I never did that," I said.

"We'll discuss the deficiencies in your childhood later," he said sensibly. "Right now you need to let go."

So I did.

He dragged me up and onto the bow of his kayak, gave me instructions about balancing with my legs, pointed out new handholds on the kayak itself, and took off his life jacket and zipped it onto me instead. The ropes slithered off the piling as he rapidly looped them into neat coils. He stuffed them down into the well beside his knees.

"Ready?"

I could only nod.

"Wind's picking up. It'll be rough. Hang on tight."

I nodded again. I'd been hanging on for what seemed like a very long time. My hands were permanently cramped in that position. I could do it for a few more minutes.

Cal removed his paddle from the clips and used it like a rudder to aim us in the right direction. Then he stroked steadily, firmly, right, left, right, left. The kayak wallowed low in the water, but he made slow, relentless progress.

We drifted the length of the wildlife refuge, dark and foreboding, water sloshing high on the muddy banks. I wondered, vaguely, where the otters nested. Nothing about the shore appeared accommodating to me. The brackish, chlorophyll taste of river water still coated my mouth, and whitecaps peaked and rippled along the sides of the kayak.

Cal didn't change course when we came to the south edge of the marina. He steered us past the *Tin Can*, looking spiffy in her new paint job. I didn't have the energy to protest. My teeth were chattering wildly, and a tremor swept the length of my body. I'd been warmer when I was mostly submerged. The wind was slicing through my clothing like a million stinging paper cuts. I might as well not have been wearing anything.

"Steady," Cal said. "Hang on." He dipped the paddle faster and veered toward *Dock's End*.

Bettina's house looked battened down. All but the sturdiest lawn ornaments and wind chimes had been removed, stored away for the season at the dramatic turn in the weather, apparently. The house seemed bleak compared to its previous vibrant excess.

Cal rapped the deck with the paddle and hollered Bettina's name. "Hold on for one more minute," he said, tying off the stern to a cleat on the deck.

I couldn't have moved if I'd wanted to.

The sliding door opened, and Bettina stepped out on the deck with a startled cry, her hand over her mouth.

"This girl needs a hot shower," Cal said.

Bettina knelt and tied the kayak at the bow. Between the two of them, they got me on the deck. I don't know how, because my limbs only flailed ineffectually. Bettina disappeared for a second and returned with a massive blanket which she snugged around me until I was a swaddled papoose somewhere in the middle. My feet poked out the bottom, and there was a little peephole for my face.

At that point, Bettina shoved Cal away. "Ladies only from here," she announced.

"I need your phone," Cal replied.

"You know where it is." Bettina guided me inside, through the living room and into the hallway, patient with my mincing steps as I pinballed off the walls. At least she didn't have to drag me. She clucked like a mother hen, pushing and prodding from behind until we were in the bathroom.

She slammed the door behind us, dodged around me to spin the faucet knobs, and started peeling me.

"Vaughn," I whispered through debilitating shivers. "I need—to—tell—him."

Bettina shoved my sweater up to my armpits. "Bend," she commanded.

I did. The sweater slid over my head and landed on the floor with a soggy splat.

"Cal can handle it," she said once she'd unhooked my bra. "Sit." She helped me ease onto the closed toilet lid and knelt to untie my boot laces.

I whimpered as she jerked on the left boot. It did not come off easily. The pain seemed to have a direct relationship with my body temperature. Now that I was warming up, the screaming pain in my ankle was shooting off the chart.

"Oh, sweetie," Bettina murmured as she rolled down my sock.

Was that my ankle? It looked like a giant log of salami, with indentations from my knit sock pressed into the swollen skin. No ankle bones in sight. I groaned.

"Shhh," Bettina cooed. "There, there."

I almost cried. I'd always wanted a mother to coddle me—with every earache, every bout of stomach flu, every sinus infection, every scraped knee and stubbed toe. And here was a sweet little lady, holding my tender ankle on her lap, making comforting sounds, trying to pretend she wasn't appalled by how grotesque it was.

I was so losing it. I blamed it on the swirling steam, which was turning the room claustrophobic and messing with my senses.

Bettina eventually got me fully undressed and propped under the shower. I clung to the soap dish for balance and carried all my weight on my solid right leg. The water streamed over my head and down my body.

I think I might have dozed. The next thing I knew, Bettina's arm had sneaked into the enclosure and she was cranking off the knobs. The stream of water stopped.

"Out," she said. She greeted me with a massive terrycloth towel and started rubbing me vigorously.

At that point, I'd recovered enough to assert my independence. It was a little surreal to be standing naked and scalded pink in front of a woman I'd known about two weeks, no matter how kind she'd been. "I got it," I whispered, clutching at the towel.

"I have nothing that will fit you properly." Bettina held up a kimono-style bathrobe by the shoulders, and I slipped my arms into the sleeves.

The silk felt dreamy against my skin, but I did, indeed, stick out in an ungainly fashion from all the openings. The cuffs dangled just below my elbows, and the hem hit me at short mid-thigh. I had a feeling the robe was close to floor-length on Bettina. But all my private parts were covered.

"Come out to the sofa." Bettina tugged on my arm. "I have an ice pack ready for you."

And that was how Vaughn found me—sprawled on his mother's sofa, draped with blankets, and my ghastly ankle elevated on a pile of pillows, encased in a drippy ice pack.

He sat on the coffee table with his knees angled in the gap between us. Cal leaned against the fireplace mantel, his arms crossed over his chest, like a sentry at ease but still vigilant, watchful.

"She's out there," I blurted.

Vaughn pitched up one brow. "Lila Halton." It wasn't a question. So he knew.

I nodded.

He reached over and took my hand, held it between both of his, ran his thumb across my knuckles. "Her car is stuck in the mud at Peregrine Pointe. From the tracks, it's clear she tried to drive away, but the problem with sports cars is they tend to be rear-wheel drive." His tilty smile was thinking about making an appearance— there at the corner. "She spun out huge ruts, but that car's not going anywhere. So she's on foot. Either hitchhiking or in the wildlife refuge."

"Or she called someone to pick her up."

Vaughn shook his head. "Her phone's not been used since she called you last night to set up the meeting." Now he grinned for real.

"You knew then?" I breathed.

The smile slipped off his face. "No. I would never have let you—no. We got her phone records late last night, as soon as Frank started talking. Even then, I only knew that she'd called you and how long you talked, not what about. But your Volvo..." He tipped his head in the general direction of the construction site upriver.

"Is stuck right beside Lila's car," I murmured.

"You know they spread gravel around at construction sites for a reason. There's a big area of gravel on the other side of the trailer. You're supposed to park..." But Vaughn trailed off when he saw my scowl.

"Wouldn't have made any difference," I said. "My keys..." I didn't have to finish. "How'd you know?" I asked instead.

"Cy Watson." Vaughn shook his head with admiration. "That kid's a marvel. I got him out of school for the day, to assist with the investigation. Thrilled him to his toes. Have you ever seen a teenage boy trying to act macho and cool and yet overcome with giddiness at the same time?"

Vaughn chuckled before continuing. "Cy and I were sitting with the forensic examiner in the lab downtown, and he was showing the examiner how his program worked and how he'd hacked into the sensor reporting system when two of the sensors up and quit right while we were watching them. One moment they're collecting data—well above the threshold Frank had specified, so Cy's program was substituting lower mercury values in real time—and the next they're dead, offline, within minutes of each other. I wondered if Frank had an accomplice out on the river destroying evidence, so I immediately called Cal and asked him to go check. He found you instead, hugging the site of the second destroyed sensor." Vaughn shrugged. "I guess I could arrest *you* for tampering with evidence."

"Don't you dare," Bettina growled from the kitchen.

I peeked over at her. She was fussing with a teapot and a plate of cookies, but it was clear she'd also been listening to every word.

I flinched as an idea hit me. "She had a paddle—or did. A paddle without a kayak." The thoughts were stringing in a loosely linear fashion now. "There's no roof rack on her car. With that car, she could never carry a kayak without a rack. When you—when the medical examiner said Ian was unconscious when he entered the water—how did he know? Did Ian have injuries? Injuries consistent with a paddle? Blows to the head or neck or something?" A vision of Lila swinging the paddle, the blade end whistling in a vicious arc, flitted through my mind and I shuddered. "When you recovered Ian's kayak, was there a paddle? I mean, I know they would have most likely become separated. They did when I—"

Cal cleared his throat from his spot against the opposite wall.

"Well, never mind," I stumbled along. "It's a big river, of course, but—"

Vaughn stopped me with a tighter squeeze of my hand. He pulled a phone out of his pocket and punched a speed dial number.

"Find a kayak paddle?" he asked the person who answered. "Uh-huh. Where? Two places? One blade broken off." Vaughn shot me a questioning glance.

I nodded. "White shaft, yellow blades. My handprint—if it's not too muddy—will be on the broken blade which I dropped about fifteen or twenty feet in from the gap in the silt fence on the riverbank."

"Where you went over the wall," Vaughn added with a squint and another hand squeeze.

I nodded.

"You left some nice tracks there too."

"I do my best," I murmured.

He muttered into the phone a few more times before hanging up—short sentences, as though he was a field general directing his troops. Every effort was being made to find the missing Lila.

CHAPTER 22

Lila was found, three hours later, soaking wet and huddling in a hollow she'd clawed into a mound of blackberry vines deep in the wildlife refuge. From all accounts, she was only slightly less miserable than I'd been. It was no consolation.

The information was relayed to me through Bettina who had also asserted her right to retrieve proper clothing from my house, help me dress, and drive me to the hospital to have my ankle X-rayed.

She also drove me home again, with a sheaf of instructions from the doctor. While my ankle was not broken, I had been told to stay off of it—and he meant *all the way* off. He'd said this most emphatically with a tremendous cinching of his bushy eyebrows into a threatening line—for at least two weeks. And after that, only tentative hobbling with the assistance of crutches. Oh, goody.

Vaughn took charge of questioning the suspects at the police station. He informed both Frank and Lila of each other's presence—in separate holding rooms—and the information began to flow fast and thick. Not all of it reliable, however. At least, not at first.

Vaughn let me proofread his report later. Said he didn't want any embarrassing typos since it was sure to be read by a lot of interested parties before the case went to court, so I examined the document with a red pen in my hand. But it was far too engrossing, and I completely forgot the guise under which I was supposed to be assisting.

I think Vaughn thought keeping me in the loop was a form of compensation for Lila's attack and my unpleasant dip in the river. He insisted on remaining under the erroneous impression that he was responsible for what had happened to me, no matter how many times I tried to talk him out of it. We had already become very good at arguing with each other.

Frank had readily admitted to the hacking by proxy. He didn't know the name of the kid he'd hired, but he'd been happy with the results. Just goofing around, he'd claimed. Nothing serious. Nobody actually got hurt, et cetera. All the classic justifications.

When Vaughn had pressed Frank about his activities on the night of Ian's murder, and he'd became aware that claiming to be with Lila wasn't going to cut it, he'd ponied up to having a meeting. A long, late-night business meeting.

Who else was at the meeting? More hemming and hawing.

"You can't have a meeting by yourself," Vaughn had said, his observation dutifully recorded in the transcript.

I chuckled.

"A couple of aides," Frank had muttered.

"Aides. Well, that's exciting," Vaughn had replied. "Aides to whom?"

"Ross Perkins."

I sat up straighter and pounded the pillow under my ankle, and maybe growled a little.

"So two aides to Ross Perkins were in the room with you?" Vaughn clarified. "How about the man himself?"

Indecipherable.

"Say that again," Vaughn insisted. "Yes or no will work."

"Yes."

On and on it went. I admired Vaughn's patience. Eventually, it came out that not only had Ross Perkins indeed been present at the meeting, but that the meeting had been called in order to come to an agreement about one of Frank's developments. And that the agreement also entailed a transfer of funds. Ross had never touched the money, but one of his aides had gone home carrying a hefty addition to his child's college scholarship fund. Frank claimed that it was just one of his many acts of philanthropy.

Vaughn was less than impressed.

Lila's interview transcript was far more emotional. She'd started babbling immediately, forgot to ask for a lawyer until she was nearly finished. Nonetheless, I couldn't help suspecting that she knew exactly what she was doing. Her story hinged on intent, and she did a very good job of claiming that everything that happened during her encounter with Ian that night had been accidental.

It was dark, she couldn't see very well. Ian wouldn't tell her what he was doing, if it was true he was seeing another woman—she'd heard rumors, but then again there were always rumors about Ian and women. His evasiveness had pushed her over the edge.

She'd known for some time that he liked to kayak on the river after dark. She thought it was a ludicrous risk, but what else would you expect from such a passionate crusader who was willing to sacrifice everything for his beloved environment? Lila continued toeing that line. In fact, she was even more effusive in her descriptions of Ian than the many eulogies that had been written about him by the faithful.

So she'd gone to the park with the long, sloping beach where he usually set off on his kayak tours and waited for him. It had been a lovers' tiff, that's all. She'd lost control, grabbed the paddle and swung it a few times. In the dark, she'd connected with some part of him, didn't know exactly where, just felt the thud shudder up the shaft to her hands.

But Ian had fallen—hard—atop his kayak. He didn't move.

She panicked. Tried to feel around for a pulse. In the dark. He wasn't breathing; she was certain. She was crying in big, gulpy sobs now. Vaughn had to stop her and ask her to repeat every other sentence so the recording would have her statement clear.

In abject horror—she actually used those words— she'd shoved Ian's kayak, with Ian on top of it, into the river. It was a stable sort of kayak, hardly bobbled as it floated away.

I wondered how she could see that. So did Vaughn, because it was the next question he asked.

Lila had to think about it for a minute. Lights on the far shore, she decided. He was silhouetted against them once the kayak was out far enough. But by that time she couldn't get him back either.

Didn't know what to do. So she carried the paddle back to her car and drove away.

"Was this during low tide?" Vaughn asked, although I was sure he knew the answer.

"I don't know. There was a lot of beach. Does it matter?"

Of course it mattered. I'd seen the fresh mud surface left behind by a receding high tide. Several feet of moving water, even if it looks calm on the surface, has amazing rearranging powers. Any signs of a struggle that might have scarred the beach at low tide would have been smoothed out within a six-hour time period, well before morning light.

"Where's Ian's car?" Vaughn asked.

"Didn't you know?" Even though I was reading the report, Lila's incredulity was evident in her phrasing. "Ian didn't own a car, hadn't for years. No fossil-fuel use for him. He was such a purist. He kept his kayak at the park, hidden in some bushes, chained to a tree. So far, no one had ever tried to steal it. Good karma or something."

Vaughn turned the conversation to Lila's employment with Cox and Associates.

Lila admitted that she and Ian had hatched the plan for her to go to work for Frank Cox so they could obtain insider information about his plans to annex the wildlife refuge. He'd offered a land exchange—a less desirable property well away from the river which he would donate to the county as a replacement refuge if they would cede the waterfront refuge to him so he could expand the adjacent development. It was a dirty proposal from the very beginning, guaranteed not to float with the county commissioners until Ross Perkins, in typical fashion, had gotten himself involved as a sort of broker.

Things had been progressing rapidly with regard to the refuge—in the wrong direction from Lila's point of view—so she'd upped the ante. Suggested a few things of a romantic nature to Frank. But it had come as a complete surprise (she claimed) when he'd taken her up on her offer the day after Ian had disappeared. She'd known he'd been at a meeting with Ross Perkins the night before and that it was something he wouldn't want to discuss with the police. The affair had been both brief and lackluster, but she'd decided to go along with it in furtherance of her cause—insinuating herself with Frank in the hope of sabotaging the land-swap deal. Which had worked perfectly because when the police came around collecting statements, Frank had asked her to back up the date of their first liaison—to claim they'd been together the night Ian went missing. In exchange for her lie, she'd extracted his promise to halt the refuge deal.

I grunted. And to cover her own little fanny. Two birds with one stone. How better to divert suspicion than to forge an alibi (for a price) with someone who needs it almost as badly as you do? Extortion, pure and simple.

I wondered, though, what must have been running through Lila's mind at the press conference, when she'd learned that she'd actually killed Ian with her second act—pushing him into the water—rather than her first act—knocking him unconscious. If she hadn't been in such a hurry to cover her tracks, her lover might have lived.

~oOo~

I was cranky. Confined. Essentially shackled to the sofa. Restless and sore. A foul mood all around. Couldn't cook. Couldn't climb the stairs to the window-lined loft. I desperately wanted to see the rain I could hear pounding on the roof.

If there was something to complain about, I found it, and obsessed upon it.

Then Sloanie brought the kids. Two giggly, bouncy girls with flyaway hair and a drooling baby who'd just sprouted his first tooth and was discovering the joys of crawling.

"Auntie Eva is going to read to you," she announced to the two girls while giving me a you-are-not-getting-out-of-this glare.

But it was one duty I had no intention of shirking, and one I was particularly well suited to fulfilling at the moment, since I wasn't going anywhere. With squeals and hasty clambering, Ginger and Hazel wedged tightly against my sides and pressed their little heads against my shoulders. I flipped pages. We read them all—Dr. Seuss, Curious George, Richard Scarry's *Busytown*, Olivia the Pig. And then we read them again. And again.

My voice was shot, but it was the best mood-lifter in the world.

In the meantime, Sloanie had tidied the house, rescued the baby multiple times when he'd gotten himself stuck in corners, stashed edibles in the fridge, opened windows for an airing, and generally spruced up the place. She'd been a blur of productivity.

A knock sounded on the door as she was bundling up the kids to leave. She opened it to Vaughn standing on the stoop, his shoulders hunched into a thick, waterproof jacket, trying to avoid the drips falling off the roof overhang.

"Welcome." She flashed him a brilliant smile, invited him in, and took his coat—the perfect hostess through and through.

But as he was wiping his feet, Sloanie shifted to winking spastically at me from behind his back, her meaning all too clear. Hazel, the three-year-old, noticed and tried to mimic her mommy. The result was grimacing facial convulsions, but she certainly gave it her best effort. I couldn't keep from cracking up.

Vaughn caught enough of the shenanigans to be concerned. "Are they always like that?" he asked after Sloanie had herded the kids out and waved good-bye.

"Yes. It's genetic. I have the same condition."

"I noticed." He settled on the sofa and stretched his legs out on the coffee table beside mine.

"Make yourself at home," I muttered. But I was glad he felt so comfortable. I got the impression it was the first time he'd truly relaxed in several days.

"How's my report?" he asked.

"Comprehensive." I pulled the pages out from under my laptop and handed them to him. "Except for one thing. Why did Lila attack me?"

Vaughn sighed. "Her lawyer's a smart guy. He got her to shut up right before we got to that part. I have a feeling he's working the temporary insanity angle, and it wouldn't look good for his client to have perpetrated two eerily similar crimes within a span of two weeks. That would suggest planning and intent."

I shook my head. "I really don't think she planned it, against me anyway. Somehow, I caught her off guard."

"Probably your comment about the mercury readings. You put her at a disadvantage because you knew something she didn't. My hypothesis is that she then assumed you knew about the murder too, when you didn't."

"Yeah, well, I figured it out pretty fast once she started swinging," I huffed.

"But if she'd been successful, disposed of you—there's no guarantee that bodies in the river ever surface, you know—she might have gotten away with it. A risk she was prepared to take, at any rate. She could have claimed you'd had an accident, slipped, went off on your own and never came back, whatever."

Vaughn wrapped a hand around mine, pulled it over to rest on his thigh, and rubbed the back of my knuckles with his thumb. It was his trademark hand-holding method, and I liked it.

"Good to see your fingers are intact," he said.

"What?" I squirmed to look at the side of his face.

But Vaughn just held my hand tighter and interlaced his fingers with mine. "That's how we knew Ian's death wasn't an accident or suicide. Defensive wounds. Three of the fingers on his right hand were broken, probably from trying to grab the paddle the same way you did while Lila was swinging it."

"Oh," I whispered. It was a sobering thought.

We sat quietly for several minutes, shoulders pressed against each other, breathing. I, for one, was enjoying being alive at that moment.

"Brought your car back," Vaughn finally said. "Got a tow truck to winch it out of the mud, and he just dropped it off in the marina parking lot."

I groaned.

"What?" He angled his body to frown down at me.

"Someday that old beast will well and truly die or get stuck and rust someplace where no one can retrieve it. It's like it has a hundred and nine lives on top of its two hundred and thirty-eight thousand miles."

Vaughn chuckled. "I know what you did for my mom, too."

I groaned again.

He elbowed me gently. "What I meant to say was, thank you."

"Anytime," I whispered. I tipped my head, rested it on his shoulder, and closed my eyes, resigned. There really were no secrets at the marina. "Who talked?"

Vaughn's voice lowered to a pleasant rumble. "I first got wind of it at the station. Karleen had to file some paperwork—the usual. She filled me in on the basics. Then I had a confidential conversation with Cal."

"Mmmm." It seemed an appropriate noise to make. I'm sure I've previously mentioned that Vaughn smells good. But it was worth noting again.

"What are you doing tonight?" he asked.

I lazily flicked my fingers at my propped-up ankle by way of friendly reminder. "Nothing."

"Not anymore. Willow called dibs on your evening. I saw her on my way down. She said to tell you that she's been practicing omelets and she's going to dazzle you with the improvement in her culinary skills. She threatened to conscript me as a taste tester too. Should I accept?"

"Mmmm," I said again, and this time I smiled.

WHAT'S NEXT

SILICON WANING
Tin Can Mysteries #2

Eva Fairchild is reveling in the idyllic, if insular, setting of her adopted home at Marten's Marina when a rash of newcomers triggers speculation and the not-so-latent nosy tendencies among the residents. Eva is appalled to learn that she's acquired a surprising new persona along with her new location—since when does she get involved with other people's problems?

But Ancer Potts' distress is not to be ignored. Everyone knows the absentminded genius needs friendly nudges now and then to get out of his shell, but Eva's certain his current trouble extends beyond the realm of social awkwardness and preoccupied introversion. And that was before he disappeared.

Eva is tossed into a sketchy, shadowy world of subterfuge when it becomes apparent that the secret project Ancer was working on is in high demand, and by dubious parties. In the race to find the missing researcher and secure the knowledge that's inside his head, Eva is forced to rely upon her new friends. But trying to explain to the handsome police detective, Vaughn Malloy, how she turned his elderly mother into an accessory to a crime could result in a real mess.

In this sedate floating community on the Willamette River, first impressions are flat-out wrong.

NOTES & ACKNOWLEDGMENTS

There are a couple real cities mentioned in this story. You will be able to find them on a map:

Portland—of course. The largest city in Oregon and site of an international airport. Even though it is not the capital, it hubs a politically and economically powerful metropolitan area that carries a lot of weight in state politics.

Scappoose—Really! The name is of Native American origin and means "gravelly plain." It's also a lot of fun to say out loud, emphatically. Rhymes with vamoose.

However, the rest of the locations are fictional (but very representative of the area where the Willamette River flows into the Columbia River).

None of the people are real, and that includes, especially, the politicians. So save your griping for the real characters, probably the ones you didn't vote for but somehow got into office anyway.

Thanks to my Airbnb host who let me experience floating-house living firsthand and who was willing to chat for a while, sharing insight into the psychological makeup of her neighbors, before she left me alone with her lovely rooftop deck and her cat. The marine community is a tight kinship. Never leave home without your floating key chain!

Thanks also to author and illustrator April Bullard, who is contagiously enthusiastic about the houseboat-dwelling lifestyle and who answered—and continues to answer—all my questions from the most basic (What happens when you flush the toilet?) to the more existential

(How do you prove your residence, and taxpaying status, when you don't have a land-based address?).

Once again, Debra Biaggi gave the manuscript her thoughtful perusal, this time on extremely short notice. What would I do without you? (Not laugh nearly so much, that's for sure.)

And deep gratitude to my mom for providing company and navigational assistance on several field trips for research purposes. We ate the results!

I claim all errors, whether accidental or intentional, solely as my own.

Deepest gratitude to *everyone* who reads my books—but most especially to those readers who take the time to post reviews online. Your comments continue to make a world of difference, not just for me as an author, but also for all the other readers out there who are considering what new mystery series to dive into.

I also have a monthly newsletter in which I share about writing progress, ask for reader input, run the occasional contest or giveaway, and just generally enthuse about books. If that sounds like your cup of tea, you can sign up at my website: jerushajones.com

SOURCES

A lot of reading goes into writing. These are some of the books, articles, and websites that inspired and informed *Mercury Rising*.

- *No Place to Hide: Edward Snowden, the NSA, and the U.S. Surveillance State*, Glenn Greenwald, Metropolitan Books, 2014
- *Citizenfour* (documentary), Laura Poitras, Radius, 2014
- *Joy of Cooking*, Irma S. Rombauer, Marion Rombauer Becker and Ethan Becker, Scribner, 1997
- 'Report: Willamette is safe for swimming, unless you're a fish', Ian K. Kullgren, *The Oregonian*, 2 December 2015
- 'Reducing Mercury Pollution in the Willamette River', State of Oregon Department of Environmental Quality fact sheet, 26 February 2007
- 'TMDL Implementation Plan for the Willamette River and Tributaries', City of Portland, Oregon, 28 February 2014
- www.willamette-riverkeeper.org
- www.rcfl.gov/northwest
- www.romancescams.org

ABOUT THE AUTHOR

Jerusha writes cozy mystery series which are set along the rivers and amid the forests of her beloved Pacific Northwest. She spends most of her time seated in front of her attic window, engaged in daydreaming with intermittent typing or pinning Post-It notes to corkboards (better safe than sorry!). She also considers maple-frosted, cream-filled doughnuts an essential component of her writer's toolkit.

She posts updates on her website: jerushajones.com

If you'd like to be notified about new book releases, please sign up for her email newsletter on her website. Your email address will never be shared, and you can unsubscribe at any time.

She loves hearing from readers via email at jerusha@jerushajones.com

ALSO BY JERUSHA JONES

Imogene Museum Mystery Series
Rock Bottom
Doubled Up
Sight Shot
Tin Foil
Faux Reel
Shift Burn
Stray Narrow

Sockeye County Mystery Series
Sockeye County Shorts
Sockeye County Briefs
Sockeye County Au Naturel
Sockeye County Skinny

Jericho McElroy Mystery Series
The Double-Barreled Glitch

Mayfield Mystery Series
Bait & Switch
Grab & Go
Hide & Find
Cash & Carry
Tried & True

Tin Can Mystery Series

Mercury Rising
Silicon Waning
Carbon Dating
Silver Lining
Lead Flying
Oxygen Burning
Iron Sinking
Neon Warning

Made in the USA
Columbia, SC
15 May 2020

97227935R00150